Wishing Well, Wishing Well

Wishing Well, Wishing Well

Jubilee Cho

Atthis Arts

Detroit, Michigan

Wishing Well, Wishing Well

Published by Atthis Arts, LLC
Detroit, Michigan
atthisarts.com

ISBN 978-1-961654-28-0

Library of Congress Control Number: 2025932408

Foreword

E.D.E. Bell

To the readers of this story —

Everyone feels emotions. Some of them are joyful, some are hard, and sometimes, they can be very hard.

As you read this story, I'd like for you to think about your feelings. What it's like to be sad, to be happy. What makes you feel both. And I'd like for you to think about your family, whoever your family is to you. Feelings, both happy and difficult, are a part of being human. When things feel hard, there are ways to get through, and ways to find your joy.

You are never alone. Even when it feels that way, you are not.

Always remember that you are beautiful and you are loved. I know this, because anyone who would read this story absolutely has something beautiful about them. And–if you're reading this book, then I love you! And if you're reading it with someone, odds are–they love you too. (And perhaps they can tell you something beautiful about you.) I also hope that you will love yourself. (Go on, tell yourself something beautiful about you; I promise you can do it.) I hope you will love who you really are. The easy parts, the hard parts, the quirky parts, and the parts people (maybe even you) don't completely understand yet.

You will learn to understand them.

And remember to reach out to people you can talk to. Family, friends, teachers, mentors, librarians, magic fairies even. (I am totally suggesting your librarians might actually be magic fairies.) Remember, you're not alone. Find the people who make you feel safe, and talk to those people: About how you feel. About what you need.

Speaking of friends, I have some wonderful ones to thank here. My gratitude and love to Ava Wu, Julia Anderson, Stella Dorohoff, Ani Dorohoff, Stewart C Baker, Minerva Cerridwen, and Patricia E. Matson for their help and care in helping this story sparkle and glitter. To Grace P. Fong for this absolutely magical cover. Jubilee would have loved it. And to Chris Bell, who trusted me, and helped guide this book along its new, unexpected, path.

Along with themes of kindness, art, and celebration, there is a theme of change in this book. That no matter how long something has been a certain way, it doesn't have to stay that way. I hope you will think about that, and carry those thoughts with you. It's ok to disagree with the characters you'll meet here, or with the society they live in, as it is with things you see in your life. Jubilee saw this story as a fairy tale, something separate from our world and its burdens, an offering of joy. I hope it brings you that joy. Yet I believe sometimes the magic of a fairy tale is to help us see things a new way, to remember that many things are possible. And that, I think, is essential to joy.

One note for such possible thought: In the kingdom of this story, people use and kill animals. I, as a vegan (someone who believes in doing what I can not to do that) encourage you, if those scenes bother you at all, to tell your own version of them. What foods would you host at your feast? How would you deal with horses, and wildlife, and farms? Your mind is your own to imagine your stories, as well.

Every writer I know loves when their stories are used to imagine new ones. To think. To create. These are the essence of our own magic.

Most importantly, hear and repeat, in whatever way you can:

Who I am, who I really am, is right.

That is what being a princess means, in this story. Perhaps you love the princesses of fairy tales, as Jubilee did, but if you prefer, think of the real royal as *you*, whoever it is that you are and will be. That crown is yours.

I hope you enjoy Jubilee's story as much as she enjoyed writing it for you.

And now, to that story—with my love and hope for each of your futures: No matter our age, each day we can write a new page.

Your friend, Emily.

Wishing Well, Wishing Well

Chapter 1:

The Grand Kingdom of Bellarossa

"—and they all lived happily ever after. The end."

The schoolchildren seated on the new library's wooden floor let out a great cheer as the girl in the front of the room closed her storybook and set it down on the chair beside her. By the doorway was the children's teacher, also smiling as she walked over to the girl, whose hand still rested on the book.

"That was wonderful, Your Majesty," the teacher said. "Class, what do we say?"

"Thank you for our new library, Princess Alexandria," the children chorused in the rehearsed timbre of school kid responses.

"You're very welcome," said the girl. "But you needn't be so formal with me. I'm not *that* kind of royal. You can call me Alex."

"Yes, of course," the teacher said as she picked up the storybook. "Forgive me, Alex. This is just very exciting. It's not every day we get visitors from the palace here in Corno Verde, you know."

Alex giggled. "I get it. It's a big day for me too. Speaking of which—" now she turned to address the whole class, "—thank you all for having me here today. It has been an absolute treat. I hope you enjoy your new library. I really do. But now, I must bid you farewell. Study with joy, and keep shining bright. The future of Bellarossa is in your hands."

The children let out another cheer before Alex took her leave, walking excitedly towards the two men seated in the lobby and surrounded by guards: none other than King Johannes Corona and Prime Minister Jean-Claude.

"Great work today," said the king, rising. "Sticking around to read to the kids after the ribbon-cutting was a nice touch."

"Thank you, Daddy!" Alex bubbled as she clutched her skirts with excitement. "I mean. I couldn't help myself. 'The Silver Swan of Crescent Lake' was one of my favorites when I was their age. I just can't *wait* for them to explore their new library! There are so many great stories in those pages just waiting to be read. I hope they love it. I know they will. Your literacy initiative will make sure of it. Right, Daddy?"

"That's right, my angel," said King Johannes. "Keep up the good work, but don't tire yourself out just yet. I'm sure your sisters will want to hear all about your special day when we get back to the palace." His face crinkled as he gave her a quick wink.

Alex flushed with pleasure as the party exited the building and settled into the carriage that sat outside the entrance to the library. She couldn't wait to tell her sisters all about the day's events. Already she was full to bursting with anticipation, and she could hardly stand it. And as the carriage ambled by, she stuck her head out the window to take in all the sights—and keep herself distracted.

The streets outside were an image taken straight from a picture book, with quaint, cobble-stone roads and red, brick buildings adorned with lush flora and handsome lampposts. Out and about were people garbed in billowy tunics, short-skirted dresses, long-tailed coats, and every other style of clothing imaginable, all dyed and embellished in a rainbow of colors. And then there were the artisans. Dozens of them—of all different crafts—bustling about as they did at all hours, not just here but in every other province of the kingdom. Musicians and dancers lost in the trance of their songs. Bakers offering free samples of brownies and cupcakes to lucky passersby. Acrobats, jesters, and magicians amazing audiences with all sorts of fantastic tricks. And hanging over the doorways of some of the artisans' shops were long, narrow trays laden with fruit and sugarcane, a time-honored practice that, according to legend, helped them create their best work.

It did Alex's heart good to see her kingdom thriving—and the people of Bellarossa were just as excited to see their princess as she was to see them. As she passed by, a trio of street magicians amidst the crowd called out to the princess.

"Happy birthday, Your Majesty!" cheered a magician. "Welcome to double digits!"

"Hope you're having a great first day of royal training," said one of her companions.

"Give your sisters our regards on behalf of Corno Verde," said the last of the three.

Alex couldn't help but glow with delight as

these lovely people lavished her with kind wishes and encouraging words. She was in a trance as she smiled and waved, until, in a snap, she heard Prime Minister Jean-Claude warning:

"Your Majesty, please, *do* be careful!"

At his words, the princess realized just how far she was leaning out the window and quickly reeled herself back into the carriage, still giddy with excitement, but more aware of her surroundings. "Oh, please, Prime Minister," she said with a grin. "You don't have to worry about me. I'm not a little girl anymore."

King Johannes chuckled. "Quite right, Jean-Claude. Alex is a big girl now. And I admit, I actually fell out of the carriage on my first day of training." He gave her another wink.

"Be glad the queen isn't around to hear you say that," quipped the prime minister.

That got a laugh from Alex and her father, and then the prime minister turned to Alex. "I suppose I can't deny that you've been doing an excellent job today. The troops in Forte Grande certainly seemed to think so. And the bishop of San Domenica."

"Mm-hmm," concurred King Johannes, as

he regarded Alex with pride. "Just think, Jean-Claude. My little girl, all grown up and starting out on her journey to become a proper stateswoman and representative of Bellarossa. I can hardly believe it myself."

Alex flushed with pride. "I'm excited too. I can't wait to tell everyone all about today. It's the first thing I'm going to do when we get back to the palace."

King Johannes chuckled, then leaned back in his seat. "Well . . . maybe not the *first* thing."

"What do you mean?" Alex asked.

"Well," said the king, his lips upturned and his eyes twinkling with merriment, "There's still one more extra special task waiting for you when we get back to the palace. A surprise to cap off your first day of royal training."

"What is it?" Alex asked, brimming with curiosity.

"Well," the king began as his smile grew even wider. "When we get back to the palace, you are going to be learning how to conduct an offering ceremony at the Faerie Well. And the best way to learn is by conducting a practice ceremony yourself."

At this, Alex gasped with delight. "Do you really mean it?" she cried, nearly jumping from her seat. "But I thought only princes were trained in that!"

"Well, yes, normally," began King Johannes. "But as you know, running the kingdom isn't getting any easier. Since I've been so busy as of late, I thought it would be a good idea to teach you how to conduct the ceremony. Someday, you'll surely have a brother, and you'll be ready to teach him when the time comes."

Alex took in her father's words and settled down in her seat, still with a smile plastered across her face. It was a little disappointing that she would never preside over a *real* ceremony, but she knew that even conducting a mock ceremony would be amazing. And as the carriage sped back to the palace, happy thoughts of overseeing her future little brother's training swirled around in her head. She hadn't even met him, yet she already loved him from the bottom of her heart. And she couldn't wait to stand beside him at the Faerie Well someday, helping prepare him to take up the family mantle of leadership.

Chapter 2:

The Newborn Prince of Bellarossa

It was getting late by the time the royal carriage rolled up to the main palace entrance after the Faerie Well ceremony, but Alex didn't seem to notice. She was far too eager to tell her sisters all about her day over dinner. Queen Soiree was regrettably unable to join them that night—a complaint of the stomach, the palace maids explained. But that still left four wonderful girls who were more than happy to welcome their father and sister home and listen as their eldest sibling told them all about her day. Alex was still regaling them well after the dessert plates were cleared, and everyone sans Prime Minister Jean-Claude had retired to one of the palace's many parlors where they could keep listening to her stories.

The parlor had an air of both comfort and elegance, perfect for sharing tales of one's triumphs. Gentle flames flickered in the hearth underneath a portrait of King Johannes's father, and around the fire were a number of handsome armchairs and sofas. Princess Lyric was lying down on a sofa with her feet propped up on the armrest. Across from her on another sofa was Princess Alamode, her legs bouncing with excitement as Princess Gateau sat by her side clutching a stuffed bunny to her chest. Occupying an armchair was King Johannes, cradling the baby, Princess Palette, to keep her from running off. And standing amidst them was Alex, still recounting her day, her sisters cheering and gasping with delight at every last detail. But Alex had saved the best for last, and nothing compared to the girls' reaction then.

"No way!" squealed Alamode. "Did you *really* get to conduct a Faerie Well ceremony? I thought only princes got to do that."

"You're *so* lucky," Lyric sighed. "I wish I could have conducted the ceremony just once before I became a princess."

"Maybe when you're ten, you can do a practice one, too," Alex said. "I can help show you."

As the girls were chattering, three of the palace chefs entered the parlor with a large platter of freshly prepared starberry tarts.

"His Majesty's favorite," said one of the chefs. "We wanted to make a special treat for such a momentous occasion."

"Thank you. That's very thoughtful of you," said King Johannes as he picked one up and took a bite. "Mm . . . they're wonderful. My compliments to the kitchen brigade."

With that, the chefs smiled and took a bow before leaving the king and the princesses to enjoy their snack. They really were delectable, the tarts. With a powerful, tantalizing aroma that wafted gently through the chamber, conjuring comfortable memories of crackling fireplaces on frosty winter evenings; of sumptuous banquets and beautifully wrapped presents; of cozy afternoons spent napping in bed; and of solitary strolls through neatly manicured rose gardens. The sweets had a calming effect on father and daughters, and as they ate, they could feel themselves relaxing after the day's exhilaration.

"Now, now, young lady, that's your fourth helping. If you eat too much just before bed, you'll upset your stomach." King Johannes's voice could be heard cautioning the young Gateau who was indeed reaching for her fourth tart.

Gateau steadied her hand and looked up at her father with imploring eyes. The king had a confused look on his face, but Lyric and Alamode's stifled giggling along with Alex's sly grin gave the game away.

"Alex, was that you?" King Johannes asked.

Alex burst into a fit of giggles with her sisters promptly following suit. Ever since she was very young, she had possessed a unique talent for mimicking her father's voice, and she was certainly not above using her gift for some lighthearted mischief.

"Last one for the night, okay?" King Johannes said, giving Gateau a smile as she happily snatched up a tart.

"Daddy?" Gateau said as she returned to her seat on the sofa.

"Yes, sweetheart?" said the king.

"Why is the Faerie Well ceremony so special?" she asked.

"Well," King Johannes began, "every year, we

hold the ceremony to offer weary, wandering faeries something to eat."

"But, but . . ." Gateau's nose scrunched up in confusion. "How do we know there are any faeries out there? No one's ever seen one."

"Well maybe not nowadays," said King Johannes. "But they used to. All the time. At least that's what the legends say."

"Tell her about the Faeries, Daddy!" Alamode gushed. "And their powers!"

King Johannes chuckled. "I will, sweetheart, I will." He turned his attention back to Gateau. "Like I was saying, according to our myths, a long time ago, humans and faeries used to live alongside each other right here in Bellarossa. They were wielders of magic, the faeries, and wondrous to behold. With radiant hair, warm smiles, and bodies that floated gently in the air. But most extraordinary of all were the magnificent wings that sprouted from their backs like butterfly wings made of stained glass. These faeries had all sorts of fantastic powers too. They were known to be able to enchant an artisan's tools to help them create their best work, but every individual faerie had their own special power on top of that. Some could conjure dancing lights. Some could make puppets dance and play. Others could talk to animals, just to name a few. Yes, they used to live alongside humans. Sharing their magic in exchange for our hospitality."

"But, but," Gateau began. "What happened? Where did they all go? Why aren't there any faeries anymore?"

King Johannes gave Gateau a kiss on the forehead. "I think that's enough questions for tonight. It's getting to be past your bedtime. Come on then. Off to bed with you."

Next to him, Alex let out a quiet sigh of relief at her father cutting the questions short. She worried, at her little sister's age, if she was ready to know the whole story.

"Up you go," King Johannes said as he scooped Gateau up in his arms. "Alex, could you get Palette?"

"Of course, Daddy," Alex said.

"Daddy?" Gateau began, once she was secured in her father's arms.

"Yes, sweetheart?" said the king.

"Do *you* believe in faeries?"

King Johannes chuckled. "Well, I suppose I

don't really know. But it's certainly fun to believe, isn't it? In any case, the royal family has always held an offering ceremony at the Faerie Well every New Year's Day. And plenty of artisans still hang trays of fruit and sugarcane over their doorways in hopes that a friendly faerie will come by and bless them for their hospitality."

"Prime Minister Jean-Claude doesn't believe in the Faeries," Lyric said plainly. "He says the legends are a lot of nonsense."

The king smiled. "Jean-Claude is a good man. But he's lacking in imagination, and if the Faeries are real, he'll be one of the last to know."

"Why, Daddy?" asked little Palette.

"Well," the king began, still smiling. "I'll tell you something, and remember this well. This world we live in is full of magic. Simply thriving with it. Magic that can be found anywhere and everywhere, but only if you have the faith to look. And, little angels . . ."

Alex knew what her father was going to say next. It was a blessing he only ever gave to his family and the prime minister. And as he did, Alex silently recited the words with him. "May you find a world full of magic."

While Alex had been looking forward to spending the rest of her childhood immersed in her training by day and her books by night, her carefree days were not meant to last. Within a fortnight of the princess-in-training's inaugural tour, the king fell gravely ill, and anxiety permeated the kingdom as the good people of Bellarossa feared for their beloved monarch's life. Minister Hopkins and her medical team tended to King Johannes day and night, but alas, as suddenly as his illness struck, death came to collect him. Following his passing, Prime Minister Jean-Claude assumed the role of regent, as was his duty as the king's premier court official. Under normal circumstances, he would have ascended the throne too, given the absence of an heir. But the day before he was to be crowned, a teary-eyed Queen Soiree emerged from her suite after a week of seclusion to announce that she was expecting a child.

Perhaps it would be a boy.

The rules were clear. If the birth of an heir was possible, passing of the line must wait.

The months ahead were difficult, grieving their father's death while awaiting the birth of a sibling, but at last, the time had come to welcome another new Corona into the world. All of the princesses were waiting impatiently outside the queen's suite where the Minister of Health and the Minister of the Heavens were alongside her for long hours. All of them wondering, would they have an heir or a girl? Soon enough, the two ministers emerged into the corridor together, Minister Hopkins cradling the princesses' new baby brother in her arms. The girls tried their best to contain their excitement so as not to wake their brother up, but in spite of the happy occasion, Alex could tell that something was amiss. For the ministers' faces were clouded with gloom, and Alex knew they had unhappy news to report.

"Minister Armstrong, Minister Hopkins, how is Mother?" Alex asked.

Minister Hopkins shifted her weight uncomfortably. "The queen . . . she . . . she's not with us any longer." She bowed her head. "I am so, so sorry."

At this, the hallway filled with the sound of five young girls crying. It just wasn't fair. They had only just lost their father. Now fate had taken their mother too? Never again would she sing them to sleep or bake them treats or read to them in the palace library. The more they considered it, the louder their crying grew. It grew so loud that they woke their brother up, and he began to cry as well. The two ministers tried desperately to console the children, and slowly, they all managed to stifle their cries, at least enough to listen.

"Your Majesties?" Minister Armstrong began once everyone had quieted. "There will be long days ahead, as you face this new life, but I can offer one small token of interest. I was able to divine your brother's affinity."

At this, the girls perked up ever so slightly. In the Kingdom of Bellarossa, every child with access to a diviner could have foretold for them an exceptional power of artistry—their "affinity," as it was termed—and even in their shock and sorrow, a newborn sibling's gift was not a moment to be missed.

"Yes," the minister continued. "The stars … they showed me … a pair of hands locked in applause, a grand auditorium filled with lights, and the famous sock and buskin—or drama masks, as you might call them. Yes … it seems the celestial bodies have foreseen that your brother's affinity be theater."

He paused for a moment as the girls turned the news over in their heads before continuing. "Of course, your brother will need a name, and Alex, it now falls on you to christen him."

At this, Minister Hopkins passed the newborn prince off to Alex, who was still sniffling.

"A name … Yes …" Alex thought out loud, marveling at the sweet new person in her arms. Did it fall to her? Then she realized she was the oldest Corona. Though she tried to keep her countenance, tears rolled again down her face.

"You should be the one to name him, Alex," Lyric reassured her, not seeming to see the new weight that had just settled on Alex's shoulders. "Words are your forte, after all." The others murmured in agreement that Alex was indeed the best suited for the task at hand.

"Thanks, everyone," Alex said with a faint blush. "Hm, all right. A name, a name, a name . . ."

As she pondered the matter before her, Alex felt the weight of tradition bearing down on her now as well. The Corona children had all been named for their affinities, and there was no reason to make their brother, already carrying the weight of heir, feel separate. When Alex was born, the minister had seen a constellation of books and paper and pens and inkwells. Thus she had been named after an ancient library in a distant land; her affinity: the pen.

Eight years ago, Lyric had been named for her affinity for song.

Six years ago, Alamode had been named for her affinity for cloth.

Four years ago, Gateau had been named for her affinity for cuisine.

Two years ago, Palette had been named for her affinity for paint.

And now, it was on Alex to come up with the perfect name for her newborn brother. She thought to herself for a few minutes, trying and discarding different names in her head, when suddenly, it came to her. "Well, with Daddy gone, there's been—you might say—a break in the Corona Dynasty. But when our brother comes of age, it'll be like the second coming of the Corona. And with his affinity being theater, I think a fitting name for him would be 'Encore'."

"Encore," mused Lyric. "You mean like when an audience asks for another performance at the end of a show?"

Alex nodded. "Yes, exactly."

"I like it," said Lyric, managing a small smile.

"So do I," said Gateau. "Prince Encore Corona."

"It's got a nice ring to it," said Alamode. "Great choice, Alex."

"Great choice, Alex!" parroted Palette.

"Yeah?" Alex asked before turning her gaze towards the little prince and smiling. "How about it, Little Brother? Do you like your name?"

At this, the newborn prince cracked a wide smile and let out an adorable coo that made his sisters' hearts melt.

"Well, I guess that settles it." Alex looked around to see a hallway full of tear-stained, yet smiling faces. "Welcome to the world, Prince Encore."

And as the newly made orphans shared a moment of mirth, they each felt as though the future might not be so bleak after all.

A few days later, Alex was sitting quietly in what had been her parents' bedchamber. She had been secretly visiting their suite every day since her mother's passing. Around her sisters and members of the palace staff, she tried to put on a brave face, but when she was alone in her parents' chamber, all her bravado melted away. And only then did she allow herself to express her grief.

"Oh, Mommy," she whispered into the bed as she ran her fingers over the sheets. "Daddy, why did you have to die? Your daughters miss you. Your son never got to meet you," she said as tears welled up in her eyes.

That's where she was, alone in her parents' enormous, empty bedchamber, when she heard the sound of approaching footsteps. Alex panicked, not wanting anyone to find her in her vulnerable state, and dove underneath her parents' bed without a second thought.

A moment later, the door opened, and in slunk Prime Minister Jean-Claude. Alex peeped out from underneath the bed and watched as he silently took a key out from his robe and locked the door. Then, he walked over to the cabinet where the late king kept his crown and removed it from its storage. Alex had to stop herself from gasping as the prime minister placed the crown atop his head and regarded himself in the mirror. He spent the next minute admiring his reflection before removing the crown from his head and putting it back in its place.

"Oh, Johannes. You just have to make this hard for me, don't you?" he chuckled. He had a twinkle in his eyes. "Fathering an heir just as you were quitting this world? I don't want to kill him. Just like I didn't want to poison you. But what choice do I have? When he's all that's standing between me and my destiny."

The prime minister sighed, his merriment never leaving his face. "Oh well, rest in peace, dear friend. In the meantime, I've a more pressing matter to tend to. Disposing of the prince. Yes . . . all I have to do is arrange for a tragic 'accident' to befall him. Then, there'll be nothing keeping me from the throne."

Underneath the bed, Alex could feel her eyes widen and her breathing quicken. She could hardly believe what she was hearing. Could it really be that Prime Minister Jean-Claude, her father's most trusted friend and confidant, had been secretly plotting to seize the throne for himself all along? Then, she had an even more horrifying thought. What did the prime minister have in store for Encore? She desperately wanted to ignore the thought but knew, deep down, that what he had said was truly his intent. She waited breathlessly for what seemed like an eternity until the prime minister left the chamber. She waited for several minutes more to make sure he was long gone, then bolted for her own suite as fast as she could.

Alex spent the rest of the day sequestered in her bedchamber. Her mind was racing and her hands were trembling as she processed what she had just witnessed.

What am I going to do? Alex thought to herself. *The prime minister was Daddy's best friend. No one would believe he would have killed him to take the throne. I saw him say it with my own two eyes, and I can hardly believe it myself.*

Alex continued to fret a little while longer before steeling her nerves. *I have to do something. What if . . . what if I requested an audience with the court? As the eldest princess who's already begun her training, they just might let me speak. And maybe . . . instead of accusing Jean-Claude, I can just convince them that the prince is in danger at home. Yes . . . and that he would be safer overseas in the care of Aunt Cinnamon in Lafete.*

Worry crept across Alex's mind once more. *They wouldn't listen to me. I'm only ten, after all. They'd probably just dismiss everything I had to say as the ramblings of a grief-stricken girl. And besides . . . I couldn't possibly speak in front of the court. All those eyes on me . . .*

In spite of her anxieties, Alex could feel a sense of duty welling up inside her. *I—I must! Little Encore's life depends on it! And words are my gift, after all. What sort of Corona would I be if I squandered my gift now, of all times!*

With that, she hurried over to her desk, pulled out a pen and some paper, and got to work figuring out what she was going to say. Her stomach felt uneasy at the prospect of speaking before the court, but she had only to think of her baby brother, whose fate lay in her pen-wielding hand, and she found the resolve to continue.

She stayed at her desk all night, outlining, drafting, and revising as necessary. She was so consumed by her task that she ended up falling asleep at her desk, and when she woke up the following morning, there were ink smudges on her hand where it had touched the paper. But she read her final draft one more time, made a last few changes, then hurried off to find Admiral Drake, her father's trusted Admiral of the Navy, to demand an opportunity to speak at the next meeting of the court. The admiral seemed slightly surprised, perhaps even amused, at Alex's boldness, but nonetheless, he promised the determined girl an opportunity to speak.

As the court was still scrambling to recover from the king's and now queen's passing, conferences were called far more frequently, and Alex's wait would not be more than a few days. And yet, the day couldn't come quickly enough for poor Alex, who felt as if she were in a daze the whole time.

Finally, the day of the conference arrived, and Alex found herself in the assembly chamber before a body of the most esteemed figures in all the kingdom. The ministers were all present, as was mandatory, but there were several provincial governors and high profile navy officers in attendance as well.

Occupying the seat just to the prime minister's right was Minister Armstrong, the most senior of the court. He had held the office of Minister of the Heavens for no less than twenty years, the longest tenure of any sitting minister, serving not only King Johannes, but also his father before him. And over those twenty years, his power to predict the unpredictable whims of fortune had made him an invaluable asset to the king, second in prestige only to the prime minister himself.

Sitting opposite Minister Armstrong was Minister Hopkins, the Minister of Health and the first woman to hold a court position in the history of the kingdom. She had once been but a humble healer operating out of a small village in Valle Panno. Though she had not had the same formal training as the palace physicians, she had made a reputation for herself as a miracle worker. And when a terrible plague was ravaging the kingdom several years ago with no signs of stopping, she had been summoned to the palace to lead the court's medical efforts and put an end to the pestilence, earning herself a seat on the court in the process.

A few seats to Hopkins's left was Admiral Drake, the only man in the navy who could claim to have evaded a fleet sailed by the Tempest, the most notorious pirate on the Bellarossian seas. The admiral was escorting a merchant convoy when the Tempest's flagship, the Grim Corsair, emerged from the fog, flanked on either side by another pirate ship. Crowning the attacking trio was the Grim Corsair's telltale obsidian flag, waving ominously in the salty sea air. Habitually, seafarers made an immediate retreat the moment they saw that infamous banner, but the Tempest's fleet—under cover of the fog—had gotten too close for that to be a possibility. With no other options, Admiral Drake had ordered his soldiers to ready themselves for battle. And though they failed to scuttle the Tempest's fleet, not a single navy vessel was lost, and over the years, tales of the battle had been elevated to a near mythic status.

And then there was Prime Minister Jean-Claude, formerly the king's right-hand man. The two had been best friends since their university days, and even back then, Jean-Claude had seemed destined for greatness. Not only had he received the highest marks in every economics, history, and political science course he took. Not only had he read a vast body of literature spanning five languages. Not only had he authored several texts that would go on to revolutionize the kingdom's fiscal policy. But he also possessed a charisma so rare that King Johannes's father—at the urging of the late university headmaster Minister Montessori as well as the then Prince Johannes—appointed him his Minister of Finance straight out of school.

As Alex regarded the prime minister, she couldn't help but feel sick to her stomach to think that such an amiable and sincere-looking visage masked such a coldhearted and treacherous villain. But she couldn't let herself get any more nervous than she already was. She hadn't even begun talking yet, but already she was praying that the quivering in her hands and legs wasn't *too* obvious.

Mitigating her anxieties somewhat was the fact that most if not all of the assembled did not appear to be offended by her addressing the court. Even though she suspected that some of them were not taking her entirely seriously, she knew that they knew how studied and sensible she was—her father had made sure of that—and they trusted her not to speak to the court frivolously. Alex was grateful for their trust.

"Go on then," said Minister Armstrong with an encouraging smile. "We're all eager to hear what the princess has to say."

"Quite right," said Minister Hopkins, her voice warm and gentle. "But let's not pressure the poor dear. Please, whenever you're ready, Princess."

"You're very brave," said Admiral Drake in a cheery tone. "Your father would be proud to see you addressing the court."

Alex nodded a silent thanks, then took a deep breath before starting. "Esteemed members of the court," she said, beginning the way she remembered her father doing so many times before. "I speak before you today to call to attention a matter of national security."

At this declaration, murmurs spread through the assembly. Several people exchanged confused looks at this grim declaration.

"Order! Order!" Prime Minister Jean-Claude called, and the court quieted down. "Princess Alexandria, you are not involved in such matters. You can be forgiven in your grief, yet our court has pressing business. You will take your seat."

Alex gulped again and felt the urge to scream at the prime minister, "I will not take my seat! You murdered him! He trusted you like a brother, and you killed him so that you could have the throne all to yourself, you venomous, rotten monster!"

But she didn't do that. Instead, she simply steeled herself and said, "Prime Minister, my involvement is not at issue, but matters that should be apparent to us all. Surely you find it strange the sudden manner in which my father passed away?"

The prime minister smiled and said, "Oh, Princess. My condolences for your loss, but people die without warning all the time. It's tragic to be sure, but not at all abnormal."

At this, Alex shook her head, for she had anticipated that the prime minister would say something to that effect. "No," she insisted. "No, it was not my father's time. You know that. I know that. We all know that. His illness came out of nowhere. Minister Hopkins, just a week before the onset of his affliction, my father was the image of health, was he not?"

At this, dozens of curious eyes turned towards the Minister of Health, and she flushed slightly, clearly not having expected to be the center of such attention.

"Um, well," the minister began. "Y-yes, I would have to say that the king's untimely passing was rather puzzling to me. As the princess says, the king was in excellent health. We know he didn't die of any sort of wound or injury. And yet, his symptoms were unlike those of any illness I've ever encountered, even in my books."

"If you feel comfortable doing so," Alex continued,

"could you tell the court if you have a theory as to the nature of my father's death?"

The minister scrunched up her face and seemed unsure of whether she should speak. "Well . . . actually—and I hesitate to make such bold statements—but when one considers the severity of his symptoms coupled with the swiftness of his demise, well, it leads me to wonder if the king may have fallen victim to some sort of poison."

At this, the murmuring returned, and now it was much louder.

"Order! Order in the court I say!" cried Prime Minister Jean-Claude. "Minister Armstrong noted nothing of this sort, and his expertise will not be maligned."

"Prime Minister, permission to speak?" asked Admiral Drake.

"Granted, Admiral," said the prime minister.

"I too must confess immense surprise at the king's untimely passing," said the admiral. "I know that I am nowhere near as qualified as Minister Hopkins to opine on the king's health, but as many of you know, the king was never one to sit idly about in his quarters on an overseas voyage. No, he preferred to help out with the operations of the ship, and to be quite honest, he was in far better condition than many of my own sailors as recently as earlier this year. And I know that I speak for many in the navy when I say that his rapid expiration came as a tremendous shock."

Alex nodded, gaining confidence as she proceeded. "And Minister Armstrong, years of training have granted you the ability to divine the will of the heavens themselves. Could you please remind the court what the stars dictated the day my father was born?"

The Minister of the Heavens was just as surprised as Minister Hopkins to be called on, but he quickly collected himself and spoke. "Yes . . . yes, I concur with Minister Hopkins and Admiral Drake. For the heavens smiled the day King Johannes—may he rest in peace—was born. Yes, I had only just started in the ministry at the time, but Minister Orion allowed me to assist him with the reading. And together we saw that the stars had bestowed a blessing of longevity onto the king. Mind you now, star reading is a constantly evolving discipline—there's still so much that is unknown. Yet if my reading is to be trusted, the king should have lived a long life absent the tampering of an external actor."

At that, the court broke out into commotion, with everyone talking all at once.

"Was there foul play after all?" mused a minister.

"It *was* quite the surprise," grumbled a governor.

"But who would want to kill the king?" cried a commodore.

"Order! I will have order in this court!" cried Prime Minister Jean-Claude as he hammered his podium with his gavel. "All right, Princess, you present a compelling argument. But as you are no doubt aware, the Ministry of Justice has already dedicated months to investigating the case of the king's death and was unable to uncover anything. What other action could you propose?"

Alex braced herself and said, "Prime Minister, my chief concern right now is my brother's safety. If someone killed my father, it's not unreasonable to think that they might target his heir next. That's why I propose we send my brother, the prince, overseas to live with his Aunt Cinnamon in Lafete until he comes of age. Many of you know Queen Cinnamon. She is a kind and devoted woman of the Corona Family. I'm sure that she would be willing to host her nephew. That way, if the threat is a domestic one, Encore will be out of their reach."

"It would be an honor to escort the prince," Admiral Drake volunteered. "While I worry for another loss for our princesses so soon, from a security position, I think it's a capital idea. Queen Cinnamon is a wonderful woman, very kind and knowledgeable in the ways of Bellarossa. I'm sure she would make an excellent guardian for the prince until he comes of age."

"I was just reading next month's forecast the other day," added Minister Armstrong. "The seas and skies ought to be in good humor, giving us the perfect opportunity to make the voyage."

"Oh?" said the prime minister. "I see. And what does the rest of the court think on the matter?"

"I think we ought to listen to the princess," called out a voice.

"Agreed," said someone else. "I move we send the prince overseas."

"As do I," said another voice. "It's too risky for him to stay in Bellarossa."

Jean-Claude swiveled toward Alex, and his voice rang clear. "And you will be happy, taking your brother away from his home? Losing the opportunity to grow up beside him?"

It was all Alex could do to contain her rage. She turned it, turned it into easy tears. "No. I will miss him every single day, yearning to see him again. But my father taught me the importance of the character of our leaders, and my brother will be raised with love, honesty, and goodwill. He will be a fine ruler, and when he returns, all the people of Bellarossa will celebrate, together."

"Very well," said the prime minister, suddenly calm. "Admiral Drake, you will be responsible for ensuring the prince's safe passage to Lafete. If that is all, court is adjourned." His tone remained agreeable, but his gaze was firmly planted on Alex. From the look in his eyes, he seemed to be trying to determine whether she was wise to his heinous deed.

She would give him nothing.

For the next week, the palace soldiers kept a close vigil over the prince as Admiral Drake bustled about making his preparations for the upcoming voyage. In addition to his flagship, the Radiance Soiree, he intended to bring four of the navy's prize battleships. Enough firepower—he was certain—to fend off any attack.

In the meanwhile, the princesses were forlorn at the prospect of being away from their brother for so long. The night before the prince was due to be sent away, they were all gathered in Alex's bedchamber, holding each other for comfort. Watching them with pain in her heart, Alex had an idea. "Here, let's write Encore a letter."

"A letter?" Palette asked.

"Yes, a letter," Alex repeated. "We can let Encore know that his sisters are all thinking of him and wishing him well. That we will see him when he is safer here."

"Good idea, Alex," said Lyric, sniffing. "Let's send off our brother with some words of love."

With that, Alex hurried over to her desk and pulled out some fresh ink and paper as well as the beautiful calligraphy set that had been the final birthday present from her father. The princesses gathered around her as they worked out what they would say. Together, they landed on the following message:

Dearest Brother, how are you? We're terribly sorry we can't be there with you right now. If you ever feel sad or lonely, please know that you are in our hearts, every single day, until we meet again. We're so proud of you for being so very brave. And we know that no matter what challenge you may face, you will stay noble and true.

Their letter complete, each of the princesses added their autograph with a flourish. Alex was just about to tuck the paper into a bottle when she noticed there was still plenty of blank space left. Her sisters watched as she wrote,

May you find a world full of magic.

"It's beautiful," said Lyric. "A message in a bottle for our dear baby brother."

"I guess I feel a *little* better now," said Gateau.

"Yeah, I'm glad Encore will have this letter," said Alamode with a thin smile.

"Me too," said Palette.

Alex sighed. "We should all get some sleep. We can hand this to Admiral Drake, ourselves, tomorrow."

The next morning, Admiral Drake was waiting at the dock for the princesses to arrive with the prince. Soon enough, they approached, escorted by a company of navy soldiers.

"Your Majesties," said the admiral solemnly. "Is the prince ready?"

"Yes, Admiral," Alex said as she handed him the basket containing the prince. "And Admiral," she said, lowering her voice, "please, whatever happens, promise me he will not set foot back in the kingdom until he is of age."

The admiral pursed his lips before nodding and giving a salute. "I give you my oath as your father's Admiral of the Navy, your brother will live to take his throne, Princess."

"Goodbye, Encore," the girls called out as they watched the Radiance Soiree carry their brother far, far away. "Goodbye, we'll miss you." While their hearts were heavy, they held close the reassurance that Encore would soon be safe in their dear Aunt Cinnamon's care.

The ships were expected to return in a month. But when six weeks passed without a single shape on the shore's horizon, everyone at the palace began to worry.

A month after that, another fleet embarked on a voyage to Lafete to learn whether the admiral had delivered his charge. A month later, the messenger fleet returned to report that the court of Lafete had never received the prince, and an emergency conference of the court was called.

"It's blasphemy!" muttered a frantic Minister Armstrong. "Complete and utter blasphemy! To think our Admiral Drake couldn't make the trip. The seas and skies were friendly the entire time!"

"Of course!" wailed Minister Hopkins. "Admiral Drake knew his way on the water better than anyone. What could have possibly overwhelmed him?"

"It certainly is a tragic twist of fate," said Prime Minister Jean-Claude with a convincing expression of solemnity. "But it's clear from your own words what claimed the lives of Admiral Drake and our dear prince."

Everyone turned to face the prime minister, who let out a great sigh.

"As you all say, even in its worst temper, the sea could never be fierce enough to get the better of our dear admiral," he said, mournfully. "We all know there's only one force on the sea that could have done so."

At this, the unhappy ministers reluctantly nodded their heads in understanding. The prime minister didn't need to name names for them to know what he was talking about. The Tempest was a merciless force of malice. Some of the assembled expressed their confusion as to *why* exactly the dreaded pirate would choose to attack a navy convoy, but then again, the squalls of the Tempest—unlike the seas—could not be divined.

"It is tragic," Prime Minister Jean-Claude repeated. "My heart aches for our dearly departed prince and heir. Admiral Drake as well. But in such times, we cannot afford to be mired in the past. We must look to the future if we're to have any hope of being the leaders that Bellarossa needs. I do not wish to take on the burdens my dear friend carried, but divine guidance is clear. Without an heir, a new line must begin. And that line must not fall to untrustworthy hands. King Johannes chose me as his closest, and so I pledge before all of you that I *will* rise to the occasion."

"What of our princesses?" Minister Hopkins asked, in a near whisper.

In silence the room waited for his answer.

"Even no longer of the divined line, they are precious to our kingdom. They will remain here, maintaining the honorary title of princess, helping to soothe the aching hearts of our people as we mend and rebuild." He lowered his head. "If no one has anything more to say, court is adjourned. Get a good night's rest, everyone. We've busy times ahead."

That night, five sad, little princesses cried themselves to sleep in their chambers. It was not the first nor would it be the last time for any of them. But none were more *despondent*, more *distraught*, more *devastated* than Alex, whose heart weighed heavy with the thought that her brother might still be alive had she not spoken up.

"—and so, it is my great honor and privilege to present to you your new ruler, King Jean-Claude!" Minister Armstrong proclaimed to the packed courtyard.

A week had passed since Encore's proclamation of death, and Jean-Claude had just been crowned king. And as Alex looked upon the former prime minister with contempt, she could only shudder to think what kind of a king he would turn out to be.

Chapter 3:

The Dark Days
of Bellarossa

"For our next order of business, I'd like to formally induct our new admiral into the court. Everyone, please extend a warm welcome to Admiral Allardyce," King Jean-Claude addressed to the hall.

A polite round of applause filled the assembly chamber as the new admiral stood up and took a bow. Admiral Allardyce was an imposing figure. A week after Admiral Drake had been pronounced dead along with the prince, she had appeared at the palace gates in an obsidian coat and a magnificent, feathered tricorne. She had come bearing a proposition: if she could do what Admiral Drake could not and vanquish the notorious Tempest, then the king would appoint her his new admiral of the navy. It seemed fair enough. In any case, no one in the navy was half as skilled a sailor, as formidable a fighter, or as charismatic a commandant as the late Admiral Drake. And so, the court agreed to her terms. But no one had actually expected her to come back a mere ten days later bearing the Grim Corsair's infamous flag. The court was skeptical at first, but after six weeks passed without so much as a single sighting of the Tempest, Allardyce was granted her promised reward.

"Thank ye, Yer Majesty," slurred the admiral, her voice soaked with brine. "I'm not much one for formalities—I'm naught but a humble mariner—but it'll be a great honor to carry out the will o' the court."

"Thank you, Admiral," said the king. "I trust that you will serve the kingdom well. On a related note, we still have yet to decide what to do regarding the recent damages to the navy fleet. As the court is no doubt aware, replacing those ships is going to cost a fortune. Each of them cost around a million fiori to build—twice that for the Radiance Soiree. But at a time like this, when the kingdom is vulnerable, maintaining a strong navy is a matter of paramount importance. Of course . . . that leaves us with the unsavory matter of recovering from this financial injury. To that end, I have conducted my own investigation, and I have arrived at the conclusion that the best course of action moving forward is to remove the tax limitations from our code. Each adult in every household will pay a weekly tax of three hundred fiori."

At this, a round of anxious murmurs swept through the court.

"Three hundred—that's absurd!" blurted out Minister Hopkins before she could stop herself. She flushed as the king turned to face her.

"Is there something you'd like to share with the court, Minister Hopkins?" King Jean-Claude asked agreeably.

"W-w-well, Prime Mini—Your Majesty, don't you find that a little . . . excessive? Rebuild the fleet, sure, but three hundred fiori? Per adult? People will lose their homes. People will starve on the streets."

"Minister Hopkins," King Jean-Claude began. "You fail to realize the grander picture. You know how much our economy depends on a strong navy. We need battleships to protect our merchant fleets. Otherwise, our cash flow freezes, and countless more will fall to poverty and starvation. We don't want that now, do we?"

"Well, well, no, I suppose not, but aren't there other avenues of raising the funds?" Minister Hopkins implored. "Your Majesty, as it stands right now, there are good Bellarossians out there struggling to earn their daily bread. I shudder to imagine what might happen with an even greater tax. Or, perhaps we could ask more of those with greater resources, or divert some of the palace funds for a time being."

"I appreciate your concerns, Minister, and I thank you for sharing them," said King Jean-Claude, his tone rich with feigned compassion. "Believe me when I tell you that it brings me no joy to levy such an austere tax. But placing an unfair burden on those who have earned the most will do nothing but cause those families to move their wealth elsewhere. And if a few hundred deaths now prevents thousands more later down the line, well, as king, it is my burden to make these difficult decisions."

"Your Majesty," said Minister Armstrong. "I concur with Minister Hopkins. As your senior minister, I must advise that we reconsider our options. May the court see the numbers?"

"Minister Armstrong," said the king, putting on a great show of patience. "With all due respect, just as I can never hope to possess your enviable power to read the heavens, please understand that it would take years of rigorous economics and social science education to comprehend the highly sophisticated principles informing my decision. Let us not forget that I previously held the office of Minister of Finance. My skill in those matters was so trusted by your former king, he took me to his side. Now, I must not let him down. I must do my duty for this kingdom."

He took a great breath before continuing, very slowly and deliberately. "Please, esteemed members of the court, I know that this is a difficult time for all of us. I know that many of you feel scared and uneasy without King Johannes here to guide us. I know because I myself often feel that way. We are a kingdom of the divine and fate has put us in this position, put me as your king. And as your king, I humbly beseech you to have the faith in me that I have in the divine plan, and in each of you beside me. Because then and only then can we step up to the challenge before us and ensure the best future for Bellarossa."

The court went silent at the king's deep and measured speech. The looks on the assembled's faces ranged from sympathetic to concerned to ambivalent. Finally, Admiral Allardyce broke the silence.

"I have faith in Yer Majesty," she announced. "He is right, ye know. I may have scuttled the Grim Corsair, but without a proper fleet to helm, well, the sea be rife with perils."

King Jean-Claude nodded. "Thank you for your trust. But I would not force anyone to remain in discomfort. Should anyone here wish to be excused from royal service, without penalty, I shall grant it immediately."

No one spoke.

"Thank you, everyone," said the king, smiling as more and more members of the assembly nodded. "King though I may be, you have stood with me today, and I want you all to know that your voices are important here. You will be called upon as needed. And for this matter, Admiral Allardyce, I am entrusting you with the duty of tax collection. Dear leaders of Bellarossa, court is adjourned."

And with that, Admiral Allardyce was dispatched out into the kingdom to carry out her foul task. Tax collection was conducted at the beginning of each season and lasted about a week. For five days, the admiral and her underlings would descend on two provinces a day, finishing off with the capital province of Corona Regis on day six. The amount they requisitioned started at three hundred fiori, but rose to six hundred, nine hundred, twelve hundred, depending on the adults of the household.

The tax wagons would rattle furiously as the royal soldiers made their way through the provinces, each cart jingling with the sound of thousands of shiny, little coins. The currency of Bellarossa was the fiore; different denominations could be distinguished by the flowers minted on them. The margherita was worth ten fiori. Four margherite made a campanula, five campanule made a rosa, four rose made a viola, and five viole made a narciso. Whatever the coin, the admiral collected it all. Those who couldn't pay in fiori paid in merchandise, livestock, or failing that, their land. Worse yet, they might also find themselves on the receiving end of the admiral's violent temper.

In fact, such a scene was presently unfolding in the forest province of Passo Legna.

"Please! You can't do this!" a young woman cried in anguish as she pushed herself up against the doors of her home.

"Sorry, lass," sneered Admiral Allardyce. One got the sense she derived some sort of morbid pleasure from her sadistic treatment of the people. "But I've orders to collect everyone's dues for the season, and since ye can't afford to pay, I'll be takin' yer tree farm instead."

"Here," she continued as she threw a sack of coins at the woman's feet. "What's left for ye after takin' what's ours. Now get lost, 'less ye want to be hauled off for trespassin' on the king's property."

"Please! This farm has been in my family for three generations!" the woman cried. "It's my home!"

But the admiral remained unmoved, and flicked her rapier, causing the woman to scramble backward and to her feet to avoid its sharp tip, crying ever harder as she stumbled, half-running, away.

"That's enough out of ye," snarled the admiral as she sheathed her blade. "Now stop wastin' my time, or by thunder, I'll not hesitate to haul ye off to the dungeon."

And with that, the admiral returned to her coach and was off to tear through the rest of the province like the merciless force of malice that she was.

The princesses—still mourning the loss of their dear parents and brother—felt their hearts ache ever more as they watched their beloved kingdom be ravaged. At first, they tried using their coin allotment to help those in need, then when they were no longer granted coins, they snuck from the palace, selling what items they could find. And now, they were relegated to the north tower, brought their meals, and kept under guard, until, the king said, they could release from their grief and regain royal composure.

Sometimes, maids were brought in to dress and style them, and to lead them to the main balcony to wave, albeit from great distance, at those gathered to hear the king's latest news and proclamations. These maids would not speak to the girls, nor were the girls allowed to speak to them, under threat of losing the day's meals.

Each and every one of them fell into a profound state of despair, and they all found themselves having great difficulty falling asleep at night.

On those nights when the princesses were up late, tormented by unhappy thoughts, Alex took it upon herself to help lull them to sleep with her power for storytelling. Such had become a nearly nightly ritual for the girls, and tonight was no exception.

On this night, Alex had just finished her self-study for the day in the tower's small library and was climbing up the stairs to the girls' usual rendezvous spot, the common chamber connecting their suites on the highest floor. Each of the girls had her own suite with a bedchamber, a parlor, a washroom, a now-barred window, and an empty chamber that would later become her creative studio. Tonight, as Alex approached the top of the stairs, she heard the commotion of angry voices locked in an argument and picked up the pace. When she made it to the entrance of the common chamber, she was greeted by the sight of Alamode and Gateau shouting at each other.

"You ruined it!" yelled Alamode.

"I didn't mean to," whined Gateau.

"For goodness sake, be quiet, both of you!" yelled Lyric as Palette was crying on one of the sofas.

"Hey, hey," said Alex from the doorway, and everyone turned towards her. "What's going on?"

"I let her borrow my dress, and she spilled juice all over it!" said Alamode as she pointed an accusatory finger at her younger sister.

"I said I was sorry," said Gateau, struggling to hold back tears. "It was an accident."

Alex ran her fingers through her hair and let out a great breath, delving deep to find her patience. Ever since their confinement here, the girls had been fighting far more frequently, and it often fell on Alex to act as a mediator.

"Gateau," she said in a gentle tone. "Don't you think you should be more careful when you're dealing with someone else's things?"

"Well," Gateau mumbled as she cast her gaze to the floor. "I guess."

"And Alamode," said Alex. "Can't you try to understand that she didn't mean any harm?"

"I suppose so," said Alamode as she clutched the skirt of her dress.

Alex watched as the two girls turned to face each other. "Now, is there something you'd like to say to each other?"

"I'm sorry I ruined your dress, Alamode," offered Gateau. "I know how much you loved it."

"I know," sighed Alamode. "I shouldn't have yelled at you."

With that, the two girls embraced as their older sisters relaxed. Off to the side, Palette was starting to calm down, and Alex walked over to pick her up and rock her gently in her arms. As she did, Lyric said, "Hey, and I'm sorry for yelling too."

"It's okay," giggled Gateau.

"We *were* being kind of a handful," admitted Alamode. "But we're okay now, thanks to Alex. She always knows what to do."

"Speaking of which," said Lyric, "I do believe it's time for something."

"Indeed it is," said Alex in her father's voice, causing her sisters to giggle. Over the past couple of months, her impression of her father turned out to have use beyond a mere parlor trick. She found that the voice was a comfort to the grieving girls, rather than a painful memory, and she had worked on getting it right, using it to lift her sisters' spirits on particularly hard nights. "Now then, whose turn is it to pick a prompt for tonight?"

"Gateau," chirped Palette.

"Right you are," said Alex. "All right then, Gateau. What'll it be?"

"Mm . . ." Gateau hummed. "Can you tell us a story about candy?"

"Candy, huh? Really changing it up now, are we?" Alex teased, eliciting a giggle from everyone. "All right then. Hmm . . . candy, candy, candy. Ah! Yes, I've got it. Are you all ready?"

Four heads nodded eagerly.

"Very well," Alex began. "It all happened in a village very far from here . . ."

Pausing her tale for the night, Alex smiled a faint, little smile as she watched her sisters sleep. Even in such difficult times, it brought Alex joy to take care of her sisters and make up stories for them. She picked Palette up to carry her off to her bedchamber. She would come back for Gateau afterwards and grab blankets for Lyric and Alamode while she was at it. When she made it to Palette's door, she turned her gaze back to her sisters and paused for a moment.

"Sweet dreams, everyone," she whispered. "May you find a world full of magic."

The Gumdrop Faerie: Part I

Somewhere, in a peaceful and prosperous village full of happy people, the children passed their days playing in the town plaza.

Known to everyone in the village was the Gumdrop Faerie. She owned a confectionery in town, but the people regarded it the way they would a magician's workshop. For the Gumdrop Faerie made the most amazing, the most fantastic, the most extraordinary sweets the world had ever seen. She spun fluffy clouds of cotton candy that were as soft as silk. She plucked rainbows from the sky and curled them into lollipops. She made chocolate bunnies that could hop over rooftops and little seeds that sprouted into candy blossom bushes. And her ice cream she made with only the freshest winter snow. The Gumdrop Faerie shared all of her wonderful creations with everyone in the village, and they all loved her dearly.

There were some children in the village that never came by the confectionary. There was Julius, a stout fellow of few words who was too nervous to be around the other children, for fear he might say something wrong. There was Amber, a lanky girl with a tic of her face and her voice. There was Nevi, a squirrely child who didn't feel comfortable as a boy or a girl. And Ike, a firecracker of a boy who was said to lack control.

As the Gumdrop Faerie looked out from her confectionery windows and saw the children peering her way on their way to school, she felt her heart ache. She knew these children were beautiful as they were, and needed to be understood, and valued just as they were. Each day, as she tended her shop, the Gumdrop Faerie tried to think of a way she could help. Then, she had an idea.

One day, there was a party and dance at the school, after class. Yet these four children walked (or in Ike's case, skipped) across the town plaza back to their homes, with backpacks laden with books and study. They were just passing by the Gumdrop Faerie's confectionery when they heard a voice call out, "Oh, children!"

The children turned to see the Gumdrop Faerie standing at the door of her shop. She wore a coral pink gown with a butter yellow sash. Her wings were sky blue.

"And where are you dears off to today?" she asked. Her voice was high and flutey.

The children, stopped for a moment, for though they were nervous if they'd done something wrong, each of them loved the Gumdrop Faerie and never wanted to upset her.

"Oh," said Amber. "I am just heading home." Her face twitched, and she turned away.

Nevi sighed. "Me as well. I never can wait to get out of this uniform."

"Another evening of not being enough," said Ike.

Julius said nothing, but glanced around nervously.

"Well, if you're looking for something fun to do, how about I give you a tour of my marvelous confectionery?" the Gumdrop Faerie suggested.

At this, the children's faces lit up.

"Are you serious?" cried Ike. "You'd really give us a tour of your confectionery? But no one's ever been behind the back door!"

The Gumdrop Faerie giggled. "I would indeed. Here, please do come in," she said as she gestured a welcome.

Chapter 4:

The Sister Princesses
of Bellarossa

The next thirteen years proved to be a miserable time for the kingdom as King Jean-Claude continued to choke every resource out of its villages. Yet none of this suffering was reflected in the stern visage of its monarch. On the contrary, as the villages grew poorer, King Jean-Claude expanded his collection of fine clothing and indulged in a sumptuous diet of meat and rare beverage.

Jean-Claude had never married, never seemed worried about his royal line or an heir to pass it to. Instead, he was often seen in the company of his admiral in the evenings, laughing loudly as they ordered trays of food and drink back to the king's suite. If, then, Jean-Claude would not have an heir, it would be the closest man to the king who would be chosen for the line someday. And so, it sent a shiver of fear through the kingdom when he named as prime minister not Minister Armstrong or anyone of the court, but one of the wealthiest men in the kingdom, a mean-spirited, unpleasant man who lived only to throw parties for those who praised him, whose many adult sons also lived in their own manors, surrounded by wealth and uncaring festivity. No one from this family surely had an interest in the throne.

All people could hope was that, someday, Jean-Claude would appoint a prime minister of some ethics and leadership. Until that day, the lights of hope continued to dim.

Yet there was a light amidst this darkness—or perhaps, rather, five lights. For as the years passed, each of the daughters of Corona grew up to become kind and compassionate young women, and each of them did what they could to make the world around them a better place.

They had learned what to say, how to speak, to be allowed, slowly, to leave the north tower and gain more freedom to travel the kingdom. Each knew that a single wrong word would be a bounty for anyone who might overhear it, whose reporting of any mention of disloyalty could be a year's food for their hungry family.

At this very moment, a hooded figure was busy at work in the forest province of Passo Legna. She was painting a mural as she had done many times prior. Her subject matter this time was the Faeries of lore. One floated amidst a flurry of colored lights. Another was surrounded by a troupe of dancing marionettes. Yet another was accompanied by a crowd of woodland critters. The Faeries were a favorite muse of hers, but that wasn't to say that her murals didn't portray a variety of subjects. Sometimes, she would paint the late King Johannes, standing tall and bathed in golden light so as to amplify His Majesty. Other times, she would paint a grown Prince Encore making his triumphant homecoming on the Radiance Soiree. In those scenes, the prince would be portrayed sporting his crown, the lost crown their father had worn, on his head as he was welcomed home to confetti and fanfare.

"Hey, Palette."

The startled artist spun around to see who had interrupted her while she was working.

"Oh, thank goodness it's only you," Palette

sighed in relief at the sight of her eldest sister. "Don't startle me like that! You almost made me mess up!" she said, eyes averted and blushing furiously over having been caught off guard.

"Hey, if you don't want to be so stressed, don't be an actual vandal," Alex teased.

"*You're* one to talk," Palette retorted. "As if what *you're* doing is any less illegal."

Alex simply giggled in response. Her younger sister was so adorable in her boldness. Alex admired her greatly.

Palette huffed, then turned her attention back to her painting. "Besides, it's not *my* fault the Prime Sinister can't appreciate great art."

Alex giggled at her younger sister's moniker for the man who had usurped the throne. As if her sisters didn't already have reason enough to loathe Jean-Claude for ravaging their beloved kingdom, their contempt for him just about tripled when Alex told each of them at the age of ten how she had witnessed him confessing to murdering their father. It was hardly surprising that amongst themselves, the princesses unanimously refused to acknowledge Jean-Claude as king. It was a small rebellion, it hurt to consider, but it was one they maintained fiercely amongst themselves.

Palette gave her work one last once-over, then motioned for Alex to take a few steps back with her. The two sisters stood in silence for a while as they each took in the splendor of Palette's latest oeuvre. Finally, Alex broke the silence.

"It really is a work of art."

It really was. And why shouldn't it be? As the princess of painting, Palette had been honing her affinity ever since she was old enough to hold a brush. Now fifteen, she had dedicated thousands of hours to the practice of all manners of painting. But her artistic education didn't end there. Over the years, she had gone on several trips to the provinces to study their regional specialties. Flower painting in the agrarian paradise of Corno Verde. Yarn dying in the weavers' workshops of Valle Panno. Glass staining in the hallowed cathedral walls of San Domenica. And printmaking right here in Passo Legna.

Alex continued to bask in the glory of Palette's painting before she let out a sigh.

"Doesn't it bother you that Jean-Claude's goons are just going to paint over it in a few days?"

"Eh," Palette shrugged. "I'm just happy to have my murals up for a little while. The people seem to love them in any case. I heard that my last one in Forte Grande drew a crowd of over fifty people at once," she said proudly. "And it gives the Prime Sinister's soldiers something to do besides harassing innocent villagers and lining their pockets with narcisi. That's a good cause if ever there was one. Besides, I'm careful. As long as I don't get caught in the act, the Ministry of Justice can't touch me."

Alex couldn't help but smile. Palette was so brave. Alex did worry about her sister's safety. The princess of painting may have grown up to be a bit of a rabble rouser, but she was also watchful and clever.

In fact, Alex would get into far more trouble herself if her activities ever became known to the king. Speaking of which, Alex realized she should be getting on her way. She had only come by to say hi to Palette before tending to her own matters in the area. And so, Alex bid her younger sister farewell with a final glance and smile at her latest beautiful, yet surely temporary, mural.

At the sea-salted shipping docks of sunny Porto Fortuna, Alamode and Gateau were engaged in their own efforts. They had arrived at the docks a couple of hours ago, leading ten colossal carts. The effort had started years ago, when the two sisters had saved some portion of the food and clothes brought to their tower and began taking it, at first under the cover of night, to villages for quiet distribution. As the news of this quickly spread with some rumor it might be two of the princesses doing it, the close-knit pair had approached Jean-Claude directly, saying they were inspired by the wonderful idea, and asking if they could run an effort to gather people's extra food or no longer needed clothes in each province and help distribute them.

Alex had been sure to mention in the company of the ever-silent maids with an unseen wink to her sisters that she was concerned the efforts would take all their time and energy, and they would not learn enough to possibly join the court someday. Still, she had been relieved when Jean-Claude granted permission, under the stipulation that only food and clothes would be gathered, as it would be improper to ask the villagers for more fiori than was already necessary.

It was something they could do, and the two put nearly all their time into the effort. They knew, however, that the items gathered were not usually extra. They were given from families also in need, but feeling they had some they could spare for others who needed it more. Occasionally, an unmarked large donation, presumably from a family of wealth who did not want to cross the king openly, would show up, as these carts had today. Gateau would sort and check the items and lead the distribution, and Alamode would meet with any village tailors who could manage to do so, providing a day of repair and mending to rent and worn garments.

None of the princesses were given fiori, but they were, perhaps in hopes to keep them busy or perhaps for Jean-Claude not to take a step too far with the court, supplied with a moderate amount of materials they could use to practice their affinity. Once thus supplied, Gateau brought loaves of bread, wheels of cheese, rolls of sausages, and jars of preserved fruits and vegetables to each distribution, and Alamode brought thick coats, cushy socks, warm gloves, knit caps, and heavy blankets.

After the first year or so, they couldn't shake the feeling that something was missing. After discussing with each other, they agreed that while nourishing food and warm clothing were no doubt of paramount importance, perhaps the situation called for a healthy dose of fun and comfort as well. And so, from that point onward, Gateau also crafted colorful candy and bundles of baked treats. And Alamode brought with her a veritable menagerie of soft, fluffy stuffed animals, filled with cleaned, shredded fabric from what remained of garments that could not be salvaged, which she offered to children and adults alike. Comforts for the hard nights, the princesses explained.

"Thank you, Princess Gateau!" a woman cried through tears as she picked up one of the baskets. "These gifts got my family through last season."

"Thank you, Princess Alamode!" called out a man, his hat lowered out of respect. "I don't know how I would have made it through the winter without a coat."

"Thank you both for taking such good care of us!" another voice proclaimed.

The two princesses smiled and waved at the crowds, their idle hands locked in each other's. They were glad to be able to contribute what they could, personally, and often reminded those gathered that they were only two of the many people involved. Yet, they remained a focus. Gateau's cooking was simply unmatched. The seventeen-year-old princess of cuisine *understood* food from the moment it was grown to every conceivable means of transforming it. She could discern which fruits and vegetables were ripe from smell alone. And, seasoned in a variety of food arts ranging from cheesemaking to pickling to meat curing, when there was an imbalance in the food gathered, she found ways to transform it into wholesome artisan meals.

Groups would gather just to see Alamode in person. Hardly a surprise. Everyone knew that she had the most admirers of any of the princesses, a fact that was in no small part due to the skill and insight given to sewing her own apparel. She *was* the princess of cloth after all, and when she *looked* good, she *felt* good. Like her sisters, she had devoted countless hours to refining her craft, familiarizing herself with the crafting of clothes, shoes, bags, and jewelry as well as with the transformative powers of hairstyling and cosmetics. She loved to radiate style and possibility while lending her hands.

"Alamode," Gateau whispered from behind where she stood, waving to the crowds. "Can we go now?"

"Oh, come on, Gats," Alamode bubbled. "I think the sight of us gives them hope. I don't know what hope there is for us, but we also can't say what the future holds. My looking nice, it's . . . a way I can show that."

"That's easy for you to say," Gateau said. "You thrive being the center of attention. You've never even had a bad hair day."

Alamode tossed her hair back with a flourish then giggled as she gave her younger sister's hand a reassuring squeeze.

"Come on, Gats," she said. "I know you're not the most comfortable making appearances before the public, but people cheer up when they see us. You wouldn't grudge them that, would you? I'm right here by your side, so just *try* not to worry too much?"

Gateau groaned inwardly but kept up her smile for the audience. "I just don't know. The bread looked a shade too pale coming out of the ovens this time. And I'm pretty sure the sausage wanted another day to cure *at least*. And the cheese—"

"Gats, stop," Alamode interrupted. "Your cooking is amazing. No one needs to be perfect, but when we're ourselves—whatever that is—we're amazing."

Gateau didn't respond.

"Look, you're beautiful as you are," Alamode continued, letting neither her smile nor her wave falter before their audience. "I know that no amount of me or Lexi or anyone else telling you that is going to convince you. But it's true. My wish is that you'll see it for yourself. But until then, we're all here to help you up when you're down. You know that, right?"

Gateau shifted her weight before giving her older sister a faint smile. "Yeah ... I know. Thanks, Sis."

Alamode gave her younger sister's hand another comforting squeeze, and Gateau squeezed back. And with that, the two sisters continued to smile and wave with a renewed sense of cheer.

In the heart of San Domenica, a crowd had gathered on the steps of Saint Zodiac's Cathedral. At the base of the stairs, Lyric had just put away her trombone and was sitting down at her harp, her audience waiting patiently for her to cast her spell over them once again. For every piece of music Lyric made was an absolute treat for the ears, transporting all who listened somewhere outside of space and time. A veritable virtuoso, Lyric had taught herself to read music before mastering the alphabet. Now twenty-one years old, she wrote her own music and was proficient in all manner of instruments. Her voice—her pride and joy—was as sweet and melodious as a nightingale's. And she was well practiced in the waltz, ballet, and the various folk dances she had learned while out in the provinces.

Years of practice were put to the test when Lyric started riding out into the provinces and making music for all who would listen. And listen the people did. For the princess of song, in spite of all the hardship, passed each day with a bit of joie de vivre. And her mellifluous melodies, imbued with her spirit of jubilation, called to mind a medley of pleasant memories. The playful babbling of a meandering brook. The bright warblings of chipper songbirds. And the assorted stirrings of the morning when the sun gently roused the world from a restful night of slumber.

Lyric had just finished tuning her harp and ran her fingers across the strings to make sure she was satisfied with the sound. She gave her audience a little smile before she began to play.

O great King Johannes, know you are in our hearts
We know that you are with us, though you had to depart
But we your loyal subjects, shall hold your mem'ry dear
And as we sing your praises, it's like you still are here

Noble, wise, and loving king, with a heart so true
We hope that you can hear our song, from beyond the blue
And if you hear us up in heaven, please smile upon us
We miss you, we love you, o great King Johannes

There were tears streaming down Lyric's cheeks as she performed the piece that had been composed as a eulogy for her late father. She usually wasn't a fan of somber, solemn songs, but she knew how much this particular ode meant to the people. Looking around, she could see many in the audience also shedding tears, no doubt pining for the long-gone days of the good king.

She did not play for the past. She played for today. For the futures that might still be. She knew there were others like her, excited to tell their families, "I am a girl," or so many other beautiful possibilities. She hoped that her presence, her smile, her beauty would give them hope.

And Lyric also knew, she sang for herself. Knowing that if she had not become a princess, Jean-Claude could not have taken the kingdom. That her brother might still be here today. She remembered what he had said, that day, her father. "Lyric, I don't know why only boys can be heirs. It's the way things always have been. But you, to be your authentic self is to be an heir to much more. To being you."

She sang. She sang for herself, for the people, for the wildest of ideas that if she could grow, learn, and change, perhaps the world could too.

Perhaps things did not need to be the way they always were.

They could be the way that made people happy.

With this moment of joy, her song brightened. She sang deeply and richly, her fingers nearly flying over the harp's vibrating strings.

The moment she finished, the audience gave a powerful ovation for their princess of song. And, as much as the people adored her music, no one dared request an encore. No one had in fact for the last thirteen years. Her heart again heavy, Lyric took her time wiping the tears from her eyes before she stood up and proclaimed, "Thank you! Thank you! I love you, San Domenica! It's always a good time playing for you all! But now it's time to say goodbye. Stay safe, and don't stop believing. I look forward to sharing more time together in love of song when I see you again."

The people let out another cheer as Lyric took a bow, and they were still making lots of noise as she sauntered over to her coach.

"If you'd like, please take the scenic route," Lyric said with a contented sigh as she laid back in her seat, her eyes closed and her lips upturned.

"I hear the wildflowers in Valle Panno are beautiful this time of year."

Meanwhile on the outskirts of Passo Legna, Alex had just arrived at an old, abandoned shack. It was a dilapidated structure, and when Alex entered, its one room interior was just as run-down as its exterior would have led one to suspect.

But off in a corner of the room, just beside a disheveled pile of dusty crates, was a trapdoor, imperceptible to anyone who wasn't already aware of it, or searching this old place from which anything of value had been long removed. And if one knelt down and tapped on the ground in a particular pattern of taps and pauses—as Alex was now doing—the door would creak open to reveal something extraordinary underneath.

It was a clandestine news press, hidden from sight of the rest of the world above. It was a humble operation, with only ten staff members and two printing presses. Altogether, they distributed just three hundred papers a week—twenty-five to each of the provinces plus fifty to Corona Regis. For now, it was enough. Even the largest provinces did not have populations exceeding a few thousand, and thanks to King Johannes's efforts, the people of Bellarossa were more literate than ever before. Twenty-five papers passed from hand to hand were plenty to inform an entire province within a day or two. And so, the Bellarossian Chronicle came to be the primary source of information amongst the people on all of the king's acts of abuse.

Alex had been writing for the Chronicle since she was sixteen. At the time, the publication had already been in circulation for a little over a year, and in that short time it had gained so much notoriety that word of it even reached the palace. One day, Palette had barged in on the girls' common chamber, wildly brandishing a newspaper. And from that moment, Alex was determined to seek the paper's source, hoping that if they would welcome her help, they'd allow themselves to be found.

For months, she roamed the provinces on the lookout for anyone who looked like they might be affiliated with the Chronicle. She kept this up until eventually, Alex came to notice a peculiar figure in Monteferro. He didn't seem to be a local. He only showed up at the end of each week, the night before the people of Monteferro woke up to their weekly papers. One night, after everyone else in the province had put out their lights, Alex was up late, observing the mysterious character as he darted from building to building, slipping papers underneath doorways. The following week, Alex approached him, fully cloaked and with cosmetics to hide her face, while he was alone at a tavern. There, she quickly introduced herself, flashed her mother's ring as proof, and asked that he take her to whomever was in charge of the press.

The courier seemed hesitant at first but took the brave risk to trust her, asking her to sit and wait in a corner of the tavern, handing her a book to read. After all of the townsfolk had put their lights out for the evening, he bid her follow him to the shack that served as the Chronicle's base of operations. The editor-in-chief was initially alarmed to see a newcomer—from the palace no less—at the press headquarters, but she relaxed when she realized Alex had come as a friend.

From that point on, Alex had been an informant and journalist for the Bellarossian Chronicle, serving as the operation's eyes and ears in the palace.

"Princess Alexandria," said the man who was peeking out from underneath the trapdoor. "One moment please," he said as he opened the door. "All right then, do come in."

"Thank you, Rowan," Alex said. "And please, there's no need for any of that 'Princess Alexandria' business with me. Just 'Alex' is fine."

"Of course, Alex," he said. "The editor-in-chief is in her office."

Alex thanked him and made her way through the maze of dingy, narrow corridors that housed the press. Evidently, the place had belonged to a gang of smugglers long ago. Or at least that was what the editor-in-chief's grandfather had told her. In any case, she had been living here ever since the king's tax collectors seized her family's tree farm thirteen years ago.

"Alex," the editor-in-chief said, looking up from her notes as Alex entered her office. Her amiable tone matched her pleasant expression. "How nice to see you."

"Good to see you too, Maple," Alex said. Then,

gesturing to the notes the editor-in-chief had been reading, she asked, "What's the damage?"

Maple sighed before reading over her notes. "Well, let's see here . . . even more are unhoused after a bad fishing season in Portebianco . . . a factory riot in Neue Ofenburg resulted in twenty-three arrests . . . even some of the smaller moneylenders in Casa Soldi are closing shop." She punctuated her words with another sigh. "Every day, a new travesty."

At this, Alex sighed as well. "As princess, it hurts me to think about all the people who are suffering. But the people need to know. I will not look away," she added in a whisper. For a moment, neither said anything, each lost in their own thoughts. Finally, Alex spoke.

"Here, my story for the week," she said as she withdrew some papers from her satchel.

"Ooh, what's the word this time?" Maple asked.

"Mm . . . bit of a slow week actually. Well, I suppose we should be grateful for that. But just a few days ago, a new motion to restore the abandoned Faerie Well was denied in court, without even the attention of Jean-Claude. No surprises there. But it is worth noting that the petition received over eight thousand signatures, far more than any previous attempt."

Maple sighed. "That's a shame. The Faerie Well ceremony would bring joy in such times."

Many had said the same to her over these years. Yet, a Faerie Well ceremony had not been held since Jean-Claude decreed the end of all royal spending on festivals and adjacent expenses some three years into his tenure.

"Our sponsorship of such events constitutes a needless and excessive burden on our treasury," the king had declared before an assembly of which Alex was part. "Please, everyone," he said to the murmuring court, "I'm not even suggesting we outlaw festivals; I understand how important they are to the people. But why should it fall on the court to eat the costs when the provinces are perfectly capable and willing to host their own celebrations?"

Of course, the provinces were in no shape to hold any but the simplest of celebrations, with their coffers running dry from the king's taxes. The ability to hold a royal festival brought together resources and strengths across the kingdom, with the ability to set up in larger spaces, and with the finest crafters of the realm. A separate concern on top of that had surfaced in Alex's head, but she was no longer allowed to speak to the court, and so she sat, watching as the court, again, gave the king another joy that should have belonged to the people.

Not that their approval really mattered. The court's function was to advise the king; he had the sole vote in every decision. Still, it remained uncanny how consistently he managed to sway the court to his side.

In spite of that, Alex had caught the king in the hallway after court had been adjourned. "Jean-Claude," she said. "What about the Faerie Well? If the court won't pay for its upkeep and conduct the annual offering ceremony, who will?"

The king had looked at her, considering whether to even answer. Ever since letting the girls free from their confinement, he had carefully balanced keeping them within his control while giving the appearance he still offered them audience, as a devoted uncle-like figure. No one in the court believed this anymore, but the act was enough to prevent anyone from raising the issue.

"No one, probably," he said. "Anyone with the

capital to finance such an operation ought to have the good sense not to waste their money on a silly, old superstition."

"But we can't just allow the well to fall to ruin," Alex had tried. "It was a wedding present from the ancestral king to his faerie bride during the height of the persecution. A promise to the Faeries, after their forest was destroyed, that they would always find sanctuary in Bellarossa if needed. If we abandon the well, what sort of message would that send?"

"Oh come now, Princess," Jean-Claude said, his voice increasingly impatient. "Even you are not serious about this. You don't honestly believe that ridiculous folk tale, do you? There's no such thing as the Fae. These faeries are nothing more than the fanciful daydreams of lazy people wanting to slack off and find shortcuts rather than be productive members of society."

"You can't be sure of that," said Alex, younger then, and still with some hopes the king might see some logic, if it went in his favor. "Why not err on the side of compassion? In case they could help you as well."

"Enough of this foolishness," the king said

sharply. "I am the king. I will not stand idly by and allow the court to throw away thousands of fiori a year on the upkeep of a glorified wastebasket, too tall even for practical use as a well. The only help I need is for you to stop wasting my time. Should I put you under increased instruction to learn royal decorum?"

"No," she said.

The king had snapped for his guards and walked briskly away. And that had been the end of it. The Faerie Well was left to fall into a state of squalor, and the kingdom's creative spirit went with it.

The people of the kingdom had not forgotten. Petitions had been sent, pleas made. They were denied now by the court, without discussion, as a matter of course. The king's position had not changed.

The fact that people still tried gave Alex so much hope. So much resolve.

"Just an absolute travesty," murmured Maple as she read Alex's notes. "All right, well thank you, Alex. Excellent work as always. The people will get to read all about it in next week's issue."

"Wonderful," said Alex. "All right, I'll be on my way then."

"Take care," said Maple. "I'll see you next week."

With that, Alex took her leave and began the journey back to the palace. Yes, though their hearts ached terribly, each of the princesses did what they could to bring light to the world around them. They'd carried on like this for years, but in spite of their best efforts, the king's avarice continued to ravage the land. It seemed as though the kingdom was doomed to suffer a regime of pain and misery.

The five sisters would never give up.

One day, a new ray of hope shone through the sadness.

It started off as an ordinary tax collection day, no different from any other. A tax convoy was on its way back to the palace, guarded by a company of boisterous royal soldiers.

"What a bouquet!" laughed one. "The people of Corno Verde are rich!"

"You mean the people of Corno Verde *were* rich," sneered another. "Not anymore."

"The king will be so pleased," gloated the captain. "I might even get a promotion."

The soldiers cheered for their captain's happy prospects and continued to boast and bluster as they went along their way. After a while, they came across a peculiar figure standing in the middle of the road. An old man garbed in an oversized cloak with a low-hanging hood that swept the ground and obscured his face. He leaned forward against a rough, knobby cane.

"Hold up!" cried the captain as he pulled back on the horses' reins. When they stopped, the captain called out, "Hail, stranger! What are you doing blocking the road? Run off, why don't you? We're in a hurry."

"Please," beseeched the old man, his voice covered in cobwebs and dust. "I ask only a simple favor. As you can plainly see, I'm old and frail. My son was a rancher in town, but he died last month. I've been trying my hardest to care for his prize horses—he was so very proud of them—but alas, they are thirsty, and I am far too weak to lead them to the river myself. Please, my stable is not so very far from here. Would you be so kind as to help a poor, old man take care of his dearly departed son's precious animals?"

"Hmm," mused the captain with a mischievous twinkle in his eye. "You don't say. Well, we can certainly help take care of them. After all, it is our duty and pleasure as servants of the king to assist a resident in need. All right, old man. Lead the way to your stable."

"Oh, thank you! Thank you!" the old man cried. "You're too kind. Here, right this way then." And he led the captain and three soldiers away from the road. His movements were slow and cumbersome, each step coming down with a dull *thud*. But eventually, they came across a small farmhouse and a stable, both very old and run-down.

"Doesn't look like a place for prize horses."

From inside came a strong *neigh*.

"I can't thank you enough," said the old man.

"Oh, the pleasure is all ours," said the captain, his eyes now alight. "After all, once we deliver your horses to the king's stables, my promotion is all but guaranteed."

"What?" said the old man, alarmed. "But, but they're my son's prized horses. You can't just take them."

"Oh? And what exactly are *you* going to do about it, old man?" asked the captain contemptuously. "You'll not interfere, 'less you want to be arrested for hindrance." With that, he led the soldiers into the stable, none of them noticing the old man latching the doors shut once they were inside. And once the soldiers were locked inside, the old man pressed his ear up against the stable door to listen.

Shortly, a horrible commotion of mad whinnying and clip-clopping hooves could be heard coming from inside the stable.

"Whoa! These beasts are mad! Forget this! Let's get out of here!" shouted one soldier, his words punctuated by a flurry of frantic footsteps.

"The doors won't open!" exclaimed another as the soldiers began to bang their fists and elbows against the locked doors.

"What?" cried the captain. "You can't be—"

The captain was cut short by a dramatic *thump*, followed by terrified screams. Three *thumps* later, the screaming stopped, and everything quieted down. The doors opened, and in came the old man, smiling under the hood of his cloak.

Inside the stable were four unconscious soldiers, strewn about unceremoniously on the ground, and four horses standing proud and tall. The old man shed his cloak, and now it was plain to see that he wasn't an old man at all, but rather a dashing boy with the unhardened features characteristic of a child having only just begun the transformation into a young man. On his feet were sandals with slabs of wood nailed underneath, the source of his added stature, the cane he held used to hold himself steady.

"Thanks, boys," said the boy with a smile as he kicked off his sandals and petted one horse on the neck. "Now for part two." With that, he undressed each soldier and arranged their suits of armor into three neat little piles. Once he was done, a vibrant, sapphire light glimmered inside his tunic, and the hollow armors assembled themselves and sprung to life, standing at attention as they awaited their instructions. Finally, the boy outfitted himself in the captain's armor.

"A little big for me, perhaps," chuckled the boy.

"But it'll have to do. All right, then! Let's regroup with the others!"

The hollow armors helped the boy lead the animals back to the road where the tax convoy was waiting.

"Captain!" one soldier called out. "That certainly took longer than we thought. We were beginning to worry. But I see you got that old fossil's horses. Nice ones, too! Excellent work, captain! The king is sure to reward us!"

"Of course he will," said the boy, imitating the captain's voice perfectly. "Now then, hand me the reins. Here, everyone who helped me collect the horses, come sit up on the cart. Everyone else can accompany on foot," he said.

With that, the boy took the reins, the soldiers who had stayed behind dismounted the tax cart to make room for the hollow armors, and the convoy resumed its journey to the palace. But they hadn't made it very far when suddenly, the air in front of them burst into a flurry of colored lights. The soldiers all screamed in surprise, but they were more composed than the horses leading the carts. The second the lights went off, the horses turned right around and ran as fast as they could in the opposite direction.

"Stop the horses, Captain!" the soldiers cried as they tried to run after the carts. But they were too slow, and soon enough, they were but tiny dots yelling in the distance as the horses ran the carts all the way back to Corno Verde.

When the convoy arrived in the town square, the people could hardly believe their eyes.

"Good people of Bellarossa!" proclaimed the boy from atop a tax wagon. "Fear not, for I am here to deliver you from the yoke of the false king! And mark my words, I shall not stop fighting until his reign of terror has come to an end!"

The people gathered quickly, in curiosity of how such a thing could be done. They lined up to receive their share of the recovered bounty and thanked their champion profusely as they did, glancing around nervously as they gathered their coin and goods.

"Oh, thank you! Thank you! Thank you!" said one woman through tears.

"I'll say!" said the next. "Someone pinch me! I must be dreaming!"

Through the cheers, another voice wavered. "Will she come here? Will we suffer for this . . . ?"

"Maybe . . . maybe we can help." Another voice pierced the sudden quiet. "With his protection?"

The boy, still glowing with pride, held up a hand. "For now, stay low. I'll move the horses into the fields, and set the carts aside. Hide what has been returned to you and tell no one where that is. I must be off. I must keep trouble moving, to turn it away from here. With that, I bid you all farewell."

Cheering and applause punctuated the boy's exit, and the people continued to rejoice long after his departure. For the auspicious scene seemed to herald the beginning of a new, happier chapter in the story of Bellarossa.

The Gumdrop Faerie: Part 2

The children followed the Gumdrop Faerie back into her shop. They followed her behind the counter and past the back door where they found themselves in an enormous corridor.

"Come on then," the Gumdrop Faerie sang. "We have so much to do and such little time. We must, of course, make sure you are home safely before supper."

The children followed their guide until she stopped in front of a colossal, red door. Above the door, in large, golden letters were the words: FRUIT FOREST.

"Ah!" said the Gumdrop Faerie. "Here we are, children! The heart of the confectionery! I hope you enjoy! I really do!"

The Gumdrop Faerie opened the door and bid the children enter.

Waiting for them inside was a simply incredible sight.

It was a fantastic forest with magnificent trees as far as the eye could see. High up in the treetops, the children could see a bounty of ripe, succulent fruit hanging from the branches just begging to be picked. Meandering through the trees was a fresh, green stream of limeade.

"What a marvelous forest!" cried Nevi as the other children gaped and stared at the extraordinary sight before them.

"Welcome to my orchard, children," said the Gumdrop Faerie. "This is where my workers grow and harvest all of the fruit we use in the confectionery."

"Workers?" asked Julius, his voice unsteady. "But no one's ever been seen going in or out of the back rooms. Surely there aren't any people working here?"

"Certainly not," said the Gumdrop Faerie. "There are no people who work here. Gnomes on the other hand . . ."

No sooner had she said that than the children noticed something strange in the treetops. Small beings no bigger than milk jugs with baskets full of fruit weaving through the branches. On the forest floor were dozens more of them carrying more fruit baskets as well as large, wooden tubs.

"Gnomes, you see, are natural gardeners,"

explained the Gumdrop Faerie. "They grow the most delicious fruit you've ever tasted, and as any chef worth their salt knows, great cooking starts with great ingredients."

"What are the tubs for?" asked Amber, still standing behind the others to hide her tic.

"Oh, they're for mashing the fruit," said the Gumdrop Faerie. "Look! There they go now!"

Sure enough, a group of five gnomes had just set down a tub near the limeade riverbank, and now they were emptying their baskets into it. Once their baskets were empty, the gnomes took off their boots, climbed in, and started jumping up and down, crushing the contents of the tub into gloop.

"See there!" said the Gumdrop Faerie. "See how they mash it up? Of course, since gnomes aren't very big, it takes quite a lot of them to get the job done. Yet, they enjoy it this way. They work together, and sing songs, and share stories of home. But once they're done, they take the gloop away to rooms all over the confectionery to be processed into all manner of delectable candies and syrups and jams."

"Gumdrop Faerie," Julius said, startling the

others, who were not used to hearing him speak, let alone twice. "Do . . . do you think that someone bigger than a gnome could mash the fruit with them?"

"Bigger than a gnome?" the Gumdrop Faerie asked with an innocent smile. "I suppose so. Why? Would you like to help?"

Julius nodded his head, and the instant the Gumdrop Faerie gave her approval, he darted off towards the gnomes. He bobbed joyfully as he asked the gnomes if he could help, and the gnomes laughed and beckoned him forward. Julius climbed into the tub and started hopping up and down like a jackrabbit, mashing the fruit with a huge grin on his face.

The Gumdrop Faerie turned to the other children and said, "It looks like our friend Julius might be a while. The gnomes will see to it that he doesn't get into any trouble. In the meanwhile, shall the rest of us carry on with our tour?"

"Oh, yes! Please!" exclaimed the children. And with that, the Gumdrop Faerie led them away, following the sparkling green river as it weaved through the forest.

Chapter 5:

The Mock Festival
of Bellarossa

Soon enough, the royal soldiers found themselves becoming painfully well acquainted with the rogue. The day after the incident in Corno Verde, he relieved another tax collection team of its hoard in Neue Ofenburg. He struck again the very next day in San Domenica. And then a fourth time in Porto Fortuna. Through their encounters with the boy, the tax collectors came to learn that he was not only a master of deception and disguise. He was not only a superlative swordsman, able to conquer the greatest fencers in the navy. No, as if that weren't enough, the boy was a veritable wizard, with the ability to channel attributes matching the Faeries of lore.

In their reports to Admiral Allardyce, the royal soldiers consistently identified three powers in the boy's arsenal. The power to conjure dancing lights. The power to bring puppets to life. And the power to communicate with animals. And with his combined strengths of wits, steel, and sorcery, there was nothing the soldiers could do to stop the boy from doing whatever he pleased.

The king's soldiers combed the nearby villages, but no one could tell them anything about the boy beyond what they already knew. No one knew where all of the stolen funds were being kept. They assured the soldiers they would stay alert.

The king doubled security on all tax convoys, but this did nothing to thwart the boy. He tried tripling it to similar effect. He even assigned a bounty: ten narcisi for his capture, dead or alive. But just as the king feared, there was no mere soldier or mercenary who could handle the boy, and so he continued wreaking havoc on the king's tax collectors. Needless to say, the boy quickly came to be hailed as the champion of the people and was fondly monikered "the Renegade Mage".

In the normally languid hillsides of Valle Panno, a crowd was clamoring outside an abandoned textile mill. On its side was a mural depicting the Renegade Mage standing triumphantly atop a mountain of narcisi, surrounded by colored lights, dancing marionettes, and a flock of animals. Standing just inside the mill was Palette, beaming with satisfaction as the people voiced their appreciation for the vibrant art.

The Renegade Mage was the talk of the town in the rocky mountains of Monteferro too. Alamode and Gateau felt that they had heard his epithet mentioned at least a hundred times while they were filling baskets, and they looked forward to hearing a hundred more. For no matter how many times they heard the people talking about what the Mage did the other day in Passo Legna or just yesterday in Portebianco, they never grew tired of seeing the way their faces lit up as they did.

Meanwhile, the sounds of guitar and excitement reverberated through the streets of Casa Soldi. Lyric was debuting a song she had written about a cat and a mouse, the sly, nimble rodent managing to constantly outwit its predator, and the crowds were wild for it. With one final strum, the princess of song concluded her performance, and she couldn't help but smile as the people whooped and cheered with delight.

All the while, the team at the Bellarossian

Chronicle was hard at work, enthusiastically reporting on the Renegade Mage's exploits.

"Incredible!" Maple gushed as she read Alex's story for the week. Alex grinned at the twinkle in the editor-in-chief's eyes. "Absolutely incredible! He's seized yet *another* convoy! And in the capital of all places! That's got to strike some fear into those tax collectors' hearts. The people of Corona Regis must have been thrilled!"

Alex smiled. "Yeah, he's really something all right."

"Really something?" Maple said. "Really something? He's a knight to surpass the king's entire court! Hey! Cedar! Willow! Stop the presses! I said, 'Stop the presses!' We've a last-minute addition before the next issue goes out!"

Alex giggled. "Well, I'm glad you're happy. I know someone who I'm sure doesn't feel quite the same way . . ."

At the palace, King Jean-Claude's wrath and frustration permeated the air like a storm cloud. The palace staff could practically sense an oncoming cataclysm as Admiral Allardyce reported the Renegade Mage's latest triumph to the king.

"Curse that wretched brat!" King Jean-Claude

nearly exploded as he crumpled up the report in his hands. "That's the third convoy he's stolen this week!"

Admiral Allardyce stood by silently as the king continued to seethe. "He's befuddling our royal soldiers, on top of it. This report is ridiculous! Conjuring up flames! Bringing puppets to life! Commanding hordes of beasts! Admiral! The discipline of our soldiers is *your* responsibility! How do you intend to get them to shape up and cut it out with all this faerie tale nonsense?"

The admiral gave the king an uneasy look and seemed to hesitate for a moment before she finally said, "Well . . . I mightn't call it nonsense."

For a moment, the king was absolutely stunned, and when he regained his senses, he roared, "What? Admiral, you can't *possibly* be serious!"

"The world be a mysterious place, Yer Majesty. Ye can only spend so much time on the water before ye start to see and hear things what make a seafarer believe in evil curses and sea monsters and restless spirits. How else do ye make sense o' the lad's witchcraft?"

"Nothing but parlor tricks. Smoke and mirrors," snorted the king. "But it doesn't really matter to me whether the boy has the help of imaginary creatures or not. All I care about is putting an end to it!"

Admiral Allardyce thought to herself for a moment before she said, "The trouble here be that ye can only assign so many troops to guard a convoy. And whenever the soldiers cross his path, it's always out on the road where the lad might've prepared any number of traps. But if ye could make him come to the palace and ambush him with the whole force o' the royal navy, well, I can't see how he makes it out of that one."

"Hmm . . ." pondered the king as he turned the admiral's suggestion over in his head. "Yes . . . set a trap for him. Lure him to the palace . . . that's it! I've got it, Admiral!"

The king calmed down before confiding his plot in the admiral. "This time of year, they used to call it Harvest Jamboree. We'll host a festival—the first in nearly a decade—to celebrate the year's bountiful harvest. Everyone will come running for such frivolity. Yes, and at the festival, there'll be a fencing tournament! With a grand prize! Ten—no, fifteen—no, *twenty-five* narcisi to the greatest fencer in the kingdom! A bouquet like that is sure to catch that greedy, cocky brat's eye. He won't be able to resist the chance to loot my coffers, nor the chance to show off his skill with steel. Yes, it's perfect! And once he's in the courtyard, we'll shut the palace gates to deny him any of his trained beasts or other tricks. We'll see how well he fares against the palace's entire security detail. Yes, have the message sent out at once!"

Admiral Allardyce nodded and with a tip of her magnificent tricorne said, "Aye, aye, Yer Majesty. It shall be done."

The very next morning, news of the festival went out to the provinces, and the kingdom was bustling with excitement. If one thing could be said about the people of Bellarossa, they were an art-loving people. If two things could be said, they were an art-loving *and* a party-loving people. For many a Bellarossian, festivals were the stuff of life, and the Harvest Jamboree had always been a particular favorite. A celebration of all things pastoral, it marked the time of year when the storehouses were at their fullest and heralded a time of good eating to come. Naturally, people's excitement exploded when they learned that they had not only the local celebrations in the provinces to look forward to, but also the first festival hosted by the court in a decade. But for many, that wasn't even the most exciting part.

"Twenty-five narcisi! It'd take years to earn that amount!" cried a farmer.

"It's quite the bouquet all right," sighed a merchant dreamily. "I could retire with that kind of money."

"Yeah, but good luck winning it," laughed a carpenter. "You'd have to be the greatest fencer in the kingdom. No one needing the money has had any time to be fencing!"

Scenes like this played out in every province of the kingdom. Even at the palace, the princesses—none the wiser to the king's heinous conspiracy—were all anticipating the festival with glee. Fueled by excitement, each of them kept busy in their creative studios, working on their own projects for the upcoming celebration. And as Alex worked at her desk, occasional snippets of Lyric's music and the scent of Gateau's culinary experiments in the background, she felt a sort of peace unlike anything she had known for the last thirteen years.

Soon enough, the day of the festival arrived. In the princesses' common chamber, the sisters were chattering with excitement for the day of revelry ahead of them.

"Whoa . . . Alamode," Lyric gasped. The princess of song couldn't help but crack a euphoric smile as she regarded the vision of beauty in the mirror before her. "Just whoa . . . I actually look like I have hips. Thank you so much."

Alamode glowed with pride as she returned Lyric's embrace. "You're very welcome, Lala. I know how those sorts of details make you feel. I hope you love your hair and makeup too. I hope you all do."

With that, a round of cheers filled the chamber. Alamode had surpassed expectations. A tribute to the Harvest Jamboree, the dresses she had crafted recalled memories of the kingdom's better years, with delicate flowers woven into everyone's expertly styled hair to match. Soft, natural makeup completed the look, doing everything it could to flatter its subject, emphasizing her best features and minimizing insecurities. And Alamode couldn't help but beam with satisfaction as she took in her sisters' delight, knowing her handiwork would provide them the confidence and comfort that would help them enjoy the party to the fullest.

"I hope you all enjoy today's feast," Gateau whispered once everyone had settled down. "The crops turned out really nice this year, and I thought I'd try out a few new recipes I've been working on."

"I'm sure everything will be delicious," Palette said, hardly able to keep still. "What *I'm* most excited about is seeing who wins the tournament."

Alex had wondered about that. Why Jean-Claude had suddenly been open to a festival, and why it involved a tournament sure to attract the Renegade Mage. Her sisters had presumed it was simply the Prime Sinister trying to gain a little favor in the light of the Mage's rebellions, but Alex felt certain the intent was for the Renegade Mage to appear.

Whether he would or wouldn't, and what might occur, Alex didn't want to let on to anyone what she suspected. She would be there to report, and had to trust this Mage knew what he was doing. If he were captured, tough choices might be ahead.

Alex smiled. "Yes, today should be a lot of fun. We all put a lot of work into our projects, and now we finally get to showcase them. Speaking of which, we should get going. It's a bit of a walk to the courtyard, and I wouldn't want to be late."

With that, the princesses made their way to the courtyard, and as soon as they arrived, they were met by two very excitable ministers.

"Ah! There you are, Princess!" said Minister Hopkins.

"Come quickly now. You're due to address the courtyard in ten minutes," said Minister Armstrong. He lowered his voice. "The king was clear you would follow his guidelines on speech."

Alex nodded. He didn't need to worry. Ever since working for the Bellarossian Chronicle, she'd not wanted to endanger her access to the palace. The fact that the king believed her finally subdued enough to let her speak in public filled her with rage, but she was the only one with the positioning that she had, and she could not give that up.

The ministers led the way to the terrace emerging from the central hall. Sitting high atop a grand staircase on both sides, the terrace offered a great view of the courtyard and was the perfect spot for delivering grand speeches and proclamations. As Alex surveyed the crowd, she could see thousands of eyes, all on her. And she didn't feel nervous in the slightest.

"Good people of Bellarossa," she began. "It fills me with a profound sense of pleasure to see so many smiles here today. Smiles . . . it seems like they've been regrettably hard to come by for a while now. I know that the last thirteen years since the death of my father and the prince have weighed heavy on many of your hearts. But you make your princess proud by showing that you have the wisdom and the courage to remember how to smile. When faced with hardship, the people of Bellarossa remember that the world is a wonderful place. And that as long as we do not forget how to smile, we will be ready to again when brighter days return. Thank you."

The princess wished, again, she could say more.

But today, they deserved this celebration. And she would never, ever give up fighting for them. As the cheers from the crowd lessened, just like that, the party got under way.

Back when he was alive, King Johannes had always been tremendously proud of the palace's unrivaled festival staff, and one look around the courtyard was enough for anyone to see that the reassembled team had not grown rusty from lack of practice. Under Palette's guidance, the decorating team had transformed the courtyard into a tableau of pastoral pride. Gallant, wooden posts held up colossal tapestries depicting picturesque portraits of bucolic life. Connecting the posts were strings of multicolored lights, and at their feet were carefully curated displays of hay bales, farming tools, scarecrows—the accoutrements of agrarian life. But the pièce de résistance was the magnificent Jamboree tree standing in the center of the courtyard, its vast network of branches adorned with a constellation of lanterns and a rainbow of ribbons.

Resting at the base of the Jamboree tree was the court orchestra, a hundred proud, their instruments of polished wood and shiny metal the tools by which they would bring the score Lyric had composed to life. Transporting their audience to billowing wheat fields caressed by sunlight, to tranquil pastures where shepherds' flocks grazed, and to lush, endless orchards thriving with fresh air and fruit blossoms. Yes, the princess of song's compositions were truly a thing of magic, and the orchestra did its part to keep her spell alive throughout the event.

But of course, the first thing everyone did after Alex's speech was *eat*. The Harvest Jamboree *was* a celebration of food after all. Dozens of tables lined the courtyard's perimeter, boasting all manner of tantalizing treats. Entire roasted animals spinning and crackling over open flames. Sizzling hot skewers of seasoned bites. Mountains of corn slathered in butter and turkey legs dripping in fat. And a whole host of sweets—cotton candy, fried dough, caramel apples—to round off the meal.

"Fantastic work, Gats!" Alamode cheered as the princesses sat down with their loaded plates. "Everything looks and smells incredible! I'll bet it tastes even better!"

"I'll say," Lyric said as she raised her chalice

in a toast. "Glorious food, Gateau. And good thing too. I'm hungry like a wolf."

"Oh yeah?" said Palette in a mock confrontational tone. "Hey, Lyric, I bet I can eat more than you."

"Slow down, you, or you're going to get sick," Alex giggled as Palette tore into her food. Then she turned to Gateau and said, "It is all excellent though. You should be very proud."

Gateau blushed at her sisters' compliments. "Thanks, everyone," she whispered. "I'm just glad you like it."

Now, the party was well and truly underway. Everywhere one looked, people were dining, dancing, and making merry. And it warmed the princesses' hearts to see their people so happy. But before long, it was time for the day's main event, and King Jean-Claude ascended the central hall terrace with Admiral Allardyce in tow to address the crowds.

"Good people of Bellarossa," he began. "I hope you are all enjoying this year's Harvest Jamboree. And now, for the day's main event: the tournament of steel. Will all who wish to participate please approach the central hall terrace?"

Before long, a crowd had gathered before the king, clamoring with excitement for the competition. There were well over fifty entrants altogether, of all different ages and sizes. Some weathered veterans with decades of experience under their belts. Some the sons of navy officers who had been training with the blade since childhood. Others still wandering mercenaries whose skills remained as of yet unknown. All of them hopeful and eager to prove themselves and walk away from the event with a fortune jingling in their pockets. None of them, presumably, wise to the king's true intentions.

Alex looked for anyone fitting the Renegade Mage's description, but for now, no one stood out.

"We will begin with a qualifying round," said the king. "For the preliminaries, competitors will square off against commissioned officers of the navy. They have been instructed to whittle down your numbers until we have only sixteen contestants remaining. Those sixteen will then compete in four rounds of sudden elimination until we have our champion. That champion will walk away with this," he said as he gestured to the large, wooden chest six soldiers had just placed at the feet of the terrace steps. The soldiers opened the chest to reveal thousands of shiny, golden fiori. The people gawked and gaped and stared in awe at a greater amount of wealth than most of them had ever beheld in their lives.

"Now then, without any further ado, let the preliminaries commence!" proclaimed the king.

The hopeful contestants roared with excitement, and with that, the preliminaries got under way. The contestants lined up at one of six stations to duel against navy officers, and it quickly became obvious who amongst the challengers were there from desperation, but ill-fit for the fast-paced spars. Ten contestants were eliminated in the first fifteen minutes; ten more fell soon after. The crowds cheered whenever someone was ousted, not only to honor their bravery, but because, with each elimination, the crowning of the champion grew ever nearer. Even the birds seemed to take an interest in the games, for a great flock of eagles had gathered in the skies over the courtyard, soaring in wide circles.

But it wasn't fast enough for King Jean-Claude, who was restlessly tapping his fingers on the terrace balustrade. "Come on! Hurry it along now!"

he called out impatiently. "We'll never have our champion at this rate."

The navy officers grew more aggressive, and one by one, more contestants were ousted until only sixteen remained. They gathered before the terrace in a neat little line as the king looked each of them over. He couldn't discern who amongst them was actually the Renegade Mage in disguise, but no matter. He'd have his answer soon enough. For now, the king smiled and offered his compliments to the remaining contestants.

"Congratulations," he said. "You've all done well to make it this far. Now, let the proper tournament commence!"

The throngs let out a great cheer as the eagles continued to circle above.

Soon, the contestants were dueling one on one for the whole crowd to see. As the air filled with the sounds of cheering and steel clashing steel, one competitor in particular caught the audience's attention. A young man with a bushy beard, garbed in brown boots and a crimson cap with a matching cape. His movements were so agile, his handling so dexterous, his power so overwhelming, it seemed almost pointless to carry on with the competition any further. Anyone could plainly see who would ultimately emerge victorious.

"What amazing technique! I've never seen anyone handle a blade so skillfully!" someone exclaimed.

"No doubt about it!" cried another. "How did he ever get to be such a master?"

"It's one heck of a show, in any case!" another voice could be heard laughing. "One heck of a show!"

King Jean-Claude took notice of the crimson-clad lad too, and a triumphant grin crept across his face. For the color of his beard didn't quite match the wisps of hair that peeked out from under his cap. The soles of his boots seemed just a bit thicker than normal, to add just a bit more height. And now there could be no doubt that the king's quarry was in his den. And though he was eager to have his prey in hand, he sat and waited for the perfect moment to spring his dastardly trap.

Fortunately, the young man did not try his patience. A thunderous round of applause marked his third victory, and once the rest of the tournament caught up to him, it was time for the championship match.

"Best of luck," he wished his fellow finalist, a silver-haired gentleman in a long, blue coat. His opponent responded with a polite nod before they both took five paces from each other, then turned and drew their blades.

The older gentleman may well have been one of the finest fencers in the kingdom next to the young man. Compared to all his previous foes, this one possessed far superior control of the blade, and much more strength and speed as well. For minutes, the two danced, the twang of blades cutting the air, and the crowd hushing to near silence. Jean-Claude watched impatiently; it didn't matter who won, but, he admitted, he hoped the boy would lose, and then be captured in his humiliation.

A crimson-clad arm flicked and swished, and a blade went careening through the air. The older man dropped to his knees as an official raised the scarlet swordsman's arm in victory. It didn't matter. Let him enjoy his victory.

King Jean-Claude smiled wickedly as the crowd erupted with excitement.

"Splendid, splendid," he said in mock admiration. "Please come forth, champion," he said, doing his best to feign an amiable tone. "Come and receive your reward."

With that, the young man sheathed his blade and started up the terrace steps. Though he was sweaty and tired, he held his head high, and there was an unmistakable spring in his step as he took in the crowds' cheers and applause.

"Congratulations on your victory," said the king. "Your skill with steel is nothing short of artful."

"Thank you, Your Majesty," said the young man, his tone courteous and jovial. "You know what they say. We people of Bellarossa strive to make an art of everything we do."

The king chuckled. "Oh, but you're a bold one, aren't you? But I suppose your confidence isn't unfounded. Your prodigious skill for dueling leads me to wonder how well you'd fare against groups."

With that, six soldiers surrounded the man and drew their weapons while dozens more in the crowd also readied their arms. The crowd could only gasp in shock and horror at the grisly scene that was unfolding before their eyes.

"There's only one civilian in the kingdom who can fence like that," the king began. "You're the

Renegade Mage, and you've been a thorn in my side for months, assaulting tax collectors, robbing the people, and disrupting the peace. Well, now I've got you. Any last words before you're hauled off to the dungeons?"

"No words," said the Mage with a twinkle in his eye. "Only this." With that, a warm, emerald light glimmered inside his tunic, and he brought both hands to his mouth to give a shrill whistle. Without a moment's delay, the droves of eagles flying overhead descended on the courtyard. King Jean-Claude could only watch—eyes wide and mouth agape—as the birds clawed at the soldiers and knocked their weapons from their hands, as the Mage bolted down the stairs to the ground below, then as twenty eagles emerged from the group and descended on the chest containing the prize money, sinking their talons into it.

"They're tryin' to fly off with the loot!" bellowed Admiral Allardyce. "Shoot down those wretched birds!"

The soldiers tried their best to comply with their commandant's orders, but with an increasing flock of birds running interference, they were having a hard enough time holding on to their weapons, much less firing them. By the point Admiral Allardyce had wrenched a rifle from one of the soldier's hands, the birds had flown off. The soldiers rushed to point their rifles, but by then, the eagles carrying the chest were long gone and the soldiers glancing in panic as if unsure what to do, whether to shoot, what might save them from the king's and admiral's wrath.

The admiral growled frightfully and scanned the courtyard for her target. Fortunately, she didn't have to look for very long before she heard a lilting voice calling out, "Oh, Admiral! Over here!"

The admiral whipped her head around to see the Mage giving her a mocking wave next to one of Palette's agrarian displays.

"There he be!" she barked, pointing her rapier at him. "Don't let him get away!"

But before the soldiers could act, there was a flash of fiery, ruby light, and a great pillar of brilliant, gold flames erupted around the Mage, concealing everything within. For a moment, the soldiers just looked on motionless, even more unsure now of what to do.

"Well, he can't stay in there forever," grumbled

the admiral as she approached the pillar. "We'll starve him out if we have to."

But there would be no need for that, for no sooner had the admiral finished her sentence than an opening formed in the column of light, and out shot a bolt of scarlet. The Mage was a determined one, all right. Even coming off of such a strenuous competition, he kept a swift pace, his crimson cape rippling in great, big billows behind him. But every which way he turned, there were soldiers waiting to deny him his escape. Completely surrounded, he turned to see Admiral Allardyce charging at him, eyes and blade gleaming.

"Take that, ye scurvy brat!" the admiral cackled as she impaled the Mage straight through the chest, much to the crowd's horror. But the admiral didn't care. She pulled her blade from his body and ran it through him several more times for good measure as her underlings cheered. Once she was sure he was good and dead, she snatched him off his feet and held him up for all to see. "Let this be a warnin' to all those thinkin' o' makin' trouble," she roared.

She shook the Mage with such rigor that his cap fell off, and the onlookers gasped in surprise.

Confused, the admiral turned to look at her victim, and what she saw shocked her. For it wasn't the Mage at all. It wasn't even a person.

It was a scarecrow.

The admiral felt herself go red in the face as she heard several people trying to stifle their laughter.

"He must have made the switch behind the fire!" cried the admiral. "Alert the gatekeepers at once! By thunder! No one gets the better o' me!" But even she knew that it was already too late. Even a minute of confusion was more than enough opportunity for the Renegade Mage to practically vanish into thin air.

By now, a crowd including King Jean-Claude and the princesses had gathered around the discarded scarecrow. "Sorcery . . ." the king could be heard muttering to himself. "Then the soldiers weren't imagining things. But that would mean—" The king growled, and stormed back up toward the steps, the admiral close behind him.

"Look!" cried Palette as she snatched up the Mage's cap and pulled a scrap of paper from inside. "It's a note!"

"What does it say?" Minister Hopkins asked.

Palette's eyes went wide, and her jaw dropped as she read the note. She opened and closed her mouth a few times, but no sound escaped. She passed the note to Alex, who was also speechless at first. But eventually, Alex managed to collect herself enough to read aloud, "To the good people of Bellarossa. May you find a world full of magic."

For most present, the words had no meaning beyond what was apparent. But each of the princesses and the king felt a great wave of realization come over them. Each of them had the same question on their minds.

Does that mean . . . ?

Before long, the tour group came across another door with a sign that read: FROSTING STUDIO.

"Ah!" said the Gumdrop Faerie. "Well, this seems as good a room as any for our next stop. Won't you all come in?"

The interior of the frosting studio looked like a giant piece of abstract art. Everywhere one looked, there were splotches of color littered across the bright, white walls. In the center of the room stood a colossal machine with any number of nozzles. Gathered around the machine were several gnomes with palettes, working the nozzles to collect all kinds of different colors of frosting. Set up around the room were several easels with gnomes hard at work painting intricate designs on large, flat sugar cookies.

"This, children, is the frosting studio," announced the Gumdrop Faerie. "This is where the gnomes paint all sorts of pretty decorations—flowers, sunrises, rainbows, you name it—on the cookies. A cookie can be delicious without color, but the gnomes insist that all of the sweets look every bit as wonderful as they taste.”

At this, Amber seemed especially interested, and even moved to the front of the group. “Gumdrop Faerie, do you think maybe I could help them paint?”

“Certainly,” said a smiling gnome who was already walking over with a cookie as well as a palette and some brushes. “The machine in the center of the room can give you frosting in any color you need.”

“Thank you!” said Amber before dashing off to the machine to select her palette, and soon enough, she was lost in her painting, thinking only of the swirls of the delicious frosting paint.

“It seems like Amber would like to stay a while too,” said the Gumdrop Faerie with a smile. “Everyone else can follow me, and we’ll continue with the tour.”

The next room on the tour was every bit as peculiar and wonderful as the previous two.

MIRACLE EGG HENS read the sign above the door. Inside the room were a hundred hens the size of swans, draped in breathtaking plumages of pink and blue. The hens were perched on tall, wooden structures, and underneath them were beds of hay for catching their eggs. The eggs themselves were fascinating little things, covered in crystals that shimmered and sparkled like fine jewelry. Dozens of gnomes wound through the room with little baskets for collecting eggs.

"What lovely hens!" exclaimed Ike, nearly bouncing in excitement.

"Aren't they?" said the Gumdrop Faerie. "They're miracle egg-laying hens. Those eggs you see make the most rich and flavorful pastries in the world. The gnomes collect the eggs and send them wherever they're needed in the confectionery. They must be collected quickly, so as to use them when their sparkle is strongest."

At this point, the Gumdrop Faerie noticed that she only saw Ike before her. She looked around and saw Nevi, peering from behind a column.

"Nevi?" asked the Gumdrop Faerie. "Are you all right?"

"I . . . I can't tell which gnomes are the boy gnomes and girl gnomes."

The Gumdrop Faerie's eyes lit up and she knelt before the child. "Magical folk do not separate into two the way that your towns still do. I'm sure they could talk to you about it, as you gather the eggs."

"Could I really?" Nevi asked, eyes wide and twinkling. A gnome, beaming with welcome, presented Nevi a basket, and with that, Nevi rushed off to collect more eggs.

The Gumdrop Faerie watched for a while as Nevi bustled about before Ike hopped on his feet, getting her attention. "Oh, Gumdrop Faerie! Could I please see the next room?"

"Of course," said the Gumdrop Faerie. "Right this way."

Chapter 6:

The Hidden Faeries
of Bellarossa

The following morning, Alex awoke to the sound of a bird rapping on her balcony window. When she got onto the balcony, she found that the bird had left behind a scrap of paper. She picked it up and read:

Meet me at the Faerie Well an hour after sundown.
– The Renegade Mage

Alex rushed to the princesses' common chamber where the others had already gathered. Each with their own scrap of paper with the same message.

"You don't suppose . . ." Alex trailed off.

"I don't know," said Lyric, knowing what Alex was thinking. "In any case, I guess we'll learn the truth tonight."

"So we're going then?" Gateau asked.

"Of course we are," said Palette. "Aren't you curious?"

"Don't be scared, Gats," said Alamode. "We'll all go together."

The sisters all agreed to head to the designated rendezvous spot that night. They went through the rest of the day in a haze until finally, the sun set, and the princesses began the walk to the Faerie Well.

It was dark when the princesses arrived, and had they not brought their lanterns, they would have had a difficult time seeing much of anything. But they almost wished that they hadn't brought their lights, for had they not, they might have been spared from seeing the Faerie Well in its pitiful state.

Back when it was cared for, the Faerie Well was a proud monument with polished stone walls ten feet tall and a handsome, wooden roof that doubled its stature. Surrounding its foundation was a wide circle of flowers in every color of the rainbow, continuous save for a single clearing upon which stood a stone pedestal.

Now, after a decade of neglect, the Faerie Well looked like something out of a ghost story, especially under the dim glow of the lanterns. A thick layer of ivy threatened to suffocate its stone walls, its roof was rotten and splintered, and the flowers surrounding it had long withered away into a gnarled labyrinth of weeds and thorns.

The princesses seemed to have made a tacit agreement not to draw attention to the well's miserable state as they each found a place to sit and wait. As they were waiting, Alex approached the pedestal before the well. Inscribed on the base was a poem which Alex began to recite to herself.

Tired, poor, hungry faeries, rest your weary souls
Come and stay; rest and repose; so that you may feel whole
We the people of this land welcome you from exile
We wish you health and luck and joy; we wish to see you smile

Take as a sign of our goodwill this majestic well
May it put to rest your fears; worries may it quell
We hope the sins of the past can give way to doves
We wish to make amends at last and offer you our love

A promise to the Faeries indeed, Alex thought to herself as she turned her gaze to the decrepit well once again. Her thoughts were interrupted when she heard Palette snap.

"Is he going to show up or isn't he?"

"He certainly is," said a playful voice. The princesses all turned to see a grinning boy pop out from behind the well. "Sorry for making you wait. And for not coming to see you all sooner. Wanted a chance to get a little more familiar with the palace grounds before I visited. I really should thank Jean-Claude for throwing that lovely little party. I had a wonderful time. Could have done with a little less attempted murder perhaps, but I'm getting off topic, aren't I? What's important now is that I finally have the chance to meet all of you . . . dear sisters."

At this, the princesses all rushed over to embrace their little brother.

"I can't believe it!" Alamode squealed. "It really *is* you! Little Cory!"

"I'm so glad you're okay!" Gateau whispered.

"Would you let your big sisters hold you?" Lyric's normally steady voice shook.

"What a way to make an entrance!" Palette

said in a rush as she gave her little brother a light punch on the arm.

"But, but, but how did you ever manage to survive?" Alex asked in disbelief.

"Oh come on, Sis," Encore said with a smile. "We finally see each other for the first time in over a decade, and *that's* the first thing you say to me?" He chuckled as his sisters let go of him. "I get it. It's only natural you would be curious. And do I have a story to tell you. You see, after you shipped me away, our fleet was sailing smoothly, when suddenly . . ."

From the crow's nest of the Radiance Soiree, the lookout could be heard announcing, "Grim Corsair at 3 o'clock! Another attacking vessel, dead ahead! They've got us surrounded, Admiral!"

On the deck below, Admiral Drake steeled his nerves. He pulled his telescope from his coat and checked the waters at 3 o'clock. Sure enough, there it was. A telltale, obsidian banner fluttering ominously over the Grim Corsair.

The admiral pinched the bridge of his nose, deep in thought. The fleet had turned around the second they caught sight of a vessel belonging to the Tempest's pirate armada, not wanting to take any chances with their precious passenger's life. But for some reason or other, the Tempest seemed intent on denying the navy their retreat, and now there were five pirate vessels forming a perimeter around Admiral Drake's fleet. And it seemed that there would be no option but to fight.

"All right, everyone!" the admiral announced. "It seems like the Tempest is rearing for a fight. So rouse yourselves for battle! The life of the prince and the fate of the kingdom depend on our victory!"

"Sir! Yes, Sir!" the crew cried.

"Stay on course!" the admiral instructed. "We'll sail straight ahead and sink the first vessel! With any luck, we'll get through before the others can catch up. Any opening they give us, we leave immediately."

The soldiers cheered as their fleet advanced towards the pirate ship, drawing closer and closer to the imminent battle. Soon enough, the ships were within firing distance of one another, and both sides opened fire. Volleys of cannonballs flew back and forth, and they were able to scuttle the closest ship, creating an opening to possibly flee.

But not without injury. For the pirates' cannon fire had ripped a hole or two in each ship's sails, drastically reducing the fleet's speed. And the pirates were in hot pursuit.

"Aim for the attackers' masts!" Admiral Drake bellowed, hoping to likewise slow down the pursuing ship.

"Sir! Yes, Sir!" the soldiers cried as they did just that. The cannoneers launched volley after volley at the attacking ships' masts and managed to slow the smaller ships, which fell back in turn. But the Grim Corsair weathered the attack, and now it was closing in on the Soiree. Soon, it was close enough that the pirates were throwing grappling hooks onto the deck of the Soiree, and now they were reeling it in.

On the Soiree's port side, Admiral Drake could see the first navy vessel beginning to sink and made a quick assessment of the situation before announcing, "I'm taking the prince with me to the shores of Corno Verde! Regroup with me there once the battle is over!"

"Sir! Yes, Sir!" the crew cried.

With that, Admiral Drake ran for the prince's quarters. As he approached, he could hear the prince crying; the commotion of the battle raging around him must have woken him up. The admiral placed the prince in his basket and bid three soldiers follow him to the lifeboats.

As the admiral emerged back onto the deck, he could see that a number of pirates had already boarded the Soiree. By now, both fleets had lost two ships, and the navy soldiers were growing frantic.

"They're ruthless!" one voice called out. "And they just keep on coming!"

"Where are the medics?" another cried in a panic. "The infirmary is overflowing!"

"We need more powder for the starboard cannons!" bellowed yet another.

When the admiral and his posse made it to the lifeboats, there were four pirates in the middle of cutting the boats free, each of whom lifted their rifles upon seeing the approaching group. The admiral swung the prince's basket behind a post, and readied his weapons along with his soldiers. Within a breath, the two parties opened fire.

Not one missed their mark. The pirates toppled into the water as the admiral's companions fell limply over the ship's side, and the admiral slammed back against the post, dealt a bullet to his core. Nonetheless, he had managed to secure one precious lifeboat, and that was all he needed.

As he stumbled into the lifeboat with the prince, Admiral Drake had to fight the impulse to scream in pain. He really would have preferred to have even *one* soldier with him—especially now that he was injured—but in this desperate situation, he couldn't risk staying aboard the Soiree a minute longer. He drew his cutlass and with one fluid motion hacked through both of the ropes holding the lifeboat up, and down they went, prince and admiral, making a great splash as they hit the water below.

Fortunately, the dark of the night and the smoke from the cannon fire gave the admiral cover to make his escape. He winced in pain as he started to row the boat, but he knew that he could not stop until the infant, in many ways, his own nephew, was safe.

He had not been rowing for more than a few minutes when he heard a massive explosion behind him. He turned to see the smoldering wreckage of the Radiance Soiree and stopped rowing for a moment, struck motionless by the thought of having lost his beloved crew and ship. But he quickly shook off the shock and resumed his task. He couldn't afford to hesitate now or else his crew's losses might all be for naught. But as he rowed, he was plagued by a worrisome thought.

What am I going to do once I make it to shore?

As it turned out, the admiral didn't end up doing much of anything. By the time he reached the shores of Corno Verde, he was unimaginably fatigued and lightheaded from exertion and his injury. The cacophonous cawing of the seagulls overhead did little to help his splitting headache. *Relentless birds*, he thought to himself. *I need to keep going . . . for King Johannes . . . for the princesses . . . for Bellarossa . . . just keep going . . . but no, I can't, no, I . . . I . . . I can't . . .* The admiral knew the situation was desperate when he started to hallucinate. For he thought he could make out three winged figures descending onto the sand before him as the world went black.

When Admiral Drake regained his senses, he found himself amongst peculiar company. Before him were three individuals who each looked to be around twenty years old. Their hair was radiant. Their smiles bright. But most extraordinary of all were the magnificent wings that sprouted from their backs like butterfly wings made of stained glass. Each one's wings shimmered in a different color—one in ruby, one in sapphire, one in emerald—and if the admiral wasn't so focused on carrying out his mission, he would have no doubt been thrilled to his core to be face to face with the Faeries of lore.

"Wh-where am I? Where's the—ah!" the admiral cried as he felt a searing pain in his side.

"Please," said the emerald-winged Faerie, concern in her voice. "Don't strain yourself. You're very injured. You might make it worse."

"Here," said the sapphire-winged Faerie as he offered the admiral a bowl of golden brew. "Drink this, it'll make you feel better."

The admiral took the bowl but did not drink. "The prince. Where is the prince?"

"Hm? Oh, if you're talking about the baby, he's safe," said the sapphire-winged Faerie as he waved towards the prince's basket, in which, to the admiral's immense relief, little Encore could be seen sleeping.

"We found both of you on the beach and brought you here," said the ruby-winged Faerie with an assured smile. "You're welcome."

The admiral nodded, still staring in gratitude at the sleeping baby. "Thank you very much."

"You should thank the seagulls," said the emerald-winged Faerie. "Clever little things. If it weren't for their cawing, we might not have found you. Oh! But where are our manners? Please, allow us to introduce ourselves. My name is Carroll."

"I'm Tanabata," said the ruby-winged Faerie.

"Drosselmeyer," said the sapphire-winged Faerie. "Please, do have some of that mead. We saved it for you."

The admiral could tell that he was in hospitable company, and he *was* desperately thirsty, so he took his eyes off of the basket and allowed himself to drink. The faerie mead was in fact the finest beverage he had ever imbibed, and as he drank, he felt his mind and body relax as his head flooded with his most cherished memories. Memories of that indescribable sense of adventure that came with exploring uncharted waters. Of the immeasurable pride he felt after each and every hard-earned victory. And of the sublime nostalgia that came over him whenever he returned to port after a long voyage overseas. He didn't stop drinking until the bowl was empty, and when he finally brought it away from his lips, he saw three faeries smiling at him with satisfaction.

"Good, isn't it?" said Drosselmeyer with an unmistakable air of pride. "Most humans never were able to get enough of that stuff back in the day."

"Really good," said the admiral. Then, realizing that he had yet to introduce himself, he said, "I'm Admiral Drake, of the Bellarossa Navy. The baby is Prince Encore, heir to the throne of Bellarossa."

At this, the faeries exchanged looks of surprise before Carroll spoke.

"When the seagulls told me that they saw a royal fleet under attack, I knew it couldn't be good.

But I never would have guessed that the prince himself was in danger."

"But," Tanabata began with a frown, "why was a royal fleet taking the newborn prince away from the kingdom?"

Admiral Drake explained about the unexplained death of King Johannes and how the court had elected to send the prince overseas for his own safety.

"The princess made me promise her not to let the prince return home until he came of age. She said he wasn't safe there until he could be crowned," the admiral said as he concluded his story. "And with the whole pirate raid affair, I see she was right! It just doesn't make any sense otherwise. The Tempest usually attacks merchant vessels, maybe passenger ships on occasion, in the interest of greed. But what could be gained from engaging a navy fleet, trying to leave? Yes, there's definitely something dubious happening here."

Carroll nodded in understanding. "I see. Yes, we heard about King Johannes's death, but we didn't know anything more than that. And I suppose in that case, returning the prince to the palace is out of the question."

The admiral nodded. "Correct. If there is foul play as I suspect, then I can't risk bringing him back. And even if I wanted to, I couldn't. Not in my current condition. But I can't make it to Lafete either without a ship or a crew."

He paused and closed his eyes. The comfort he had gotten from the faerie mead had all but dissipated, and now he was wracked with worry once more. After a few moments, he opened his eyes again. "I haven't got much life left in me. But I must ensure the prince's safety."

The trio regarded the admiral with sympathy. Then Carroll had an idea.

"Well," she began, "what if we took care of the prince until he came of age?"

At this, Drosselmeyer and Tanabata's faces lit up.

"You can't be serious," said Admiral Drake. "You would spend the next eighteen years taking care of the prince?"

"Well, let's see," said Carroll with a smile as she turned to the others. "What do you two think?"

"Do you even have to ask?" said Tanabata.

"Sounds like fun," said Drosselmeyer.

Carroll giggled before she turned to the

admiral. "You see, Admiral, many faeries—the three of us included—hold the royal family in the highest regard. The Corona have always been mindful to leave us offerings at the Faerie Well, and King Johannes was known to be kind, and always mean well, if a bit blocked by the past. It would be a great honor and a privilege for us to rear the prince."

The admiral looked around at three bright and eager faces. He thought about the situation for a moment, then nodded. "You'll find his crown, recently his father's crown, in his basket. Show that to the court when you bring him back. As for now, you have my sincerest thanks. The Kingdom of Bellarossa is in your debt."

Though they tried to heal him of his injuries, the admiral soon passed away, and the faeries made him a little memorial in the woods. They regretted not being able to give him a more grandiose resting place, but that only strengthened their resolve to carry out his dying wish to ensure the prince's safety.

And so, the faeries took the infant prince to their camp in the woods where he would be safe from anyone who would wish him harm. Over the following years, they took care of the boy as their own. Whatever they needed, they could gather in the forest or purchase from the nearby human settlement in Corno Verde with the money they made posing as street magicians. To the best of their ability, they made sure the boy got a good education, teaching him to read and write and do arithmetic as well as making sure he had a strong foundation in the history and current affairs of both Human and Fae nations. And they brought him all sorts of toys and treats from the human town, and put on wonderful shows for him with their fantastic powers. But all the while, they withheld from him knowledge of his true identity and the role he could someday play in the story of Bellarossa. They thought it best that not even he know the truth. Still, they feared for his safety, and just to make absolutely sure he could not be discovered, they forbade him from ever venturing to the human settlement or having any sort of contact with humans.

"But why *can't* I go with you?" he asked one day

as Carroll and Tanabata were donning the cloaks they wore to conceal their wings whenever they went into town for supplies.

"Enrico," said Carroll, using the alias they had given him. "We've told you a hundred times. Your parents were notorious. If you go into town, someone might recognize you and lock you away forever. The night before your parents were taken in, they entrusted us, your faerie godparents, with your safety. It was their final wish. Do you understand?"

Little Enrico nodded but was still frowning. "Humans sure are terrible."

"Hey now," said Drosselmeyer. "Don't say that."

"Why not? They'd put me in prison when I didn't even do anything. Not to mention all the bad stuff they did to the faeries," Enrico pouted. "Tanabata told me all about it."

At this, Carroll and Drosselmeyer shot Tanabata disapproving looks, which the ruby-winged Faerie returned with defiantly pursed lips.

Carroll turned her attention back to Enrico and gave his shoulder a comforting squeeze. "Well, it's certainly true that there are horrible people out there, but think of all the kind people who leave offerings for us, who try to help others. There will be a day you can rejoin them again, and see for yourself."

"And there's all the amazing stuff humans make," Drosselmeyer added. "Look at all your lovely toys and storybooks. And the delicious treats we bring back from town. All made by humans. Now you don't think that the people who make such wonderful things could be all bad, do you?"

"I guess not . . ." Enrico said.

"Whatever," Tanabata snorted. "I am not interested in excusing humans for their murders."

"Says the Faerie who uses her lights to guide lost travelers to safety," said Drosselmeyer with a tilt of his head. "We are not excusing them," he said as much to Tanabata as Enrico. "But we will not participate in spreading fear for a society, the way some humans did, that caused the near-destruction of ours. Our path to hope is knowing that human nature is kindness. It is when some want more at the expense of others that harm grows. But more people are kind than greedy. Humans will find their way, their power in working together. I am sure of it."

In the resulting silence, Carroll turned to

Enrico and smiled. "Enrico, please wait to decide yourself about the Humans. When you're older and won't be locked away, we'll take you to meet people, I promise. And you'll see for yourself just how wonderful they can be. Until then, promise us you'll stay hidden in the forest?"

On the inside, Enrico sighed with disappointment, but on the outside, he managed a faint smile. "Okay. I promise."

Carroll smiled and gave Enrico a tender hug. "Thank you for understanding, Enrico. Here. How about you get in some fencing practice with Drosselmeyer? Then, when we get back, we can put on a special show for you? As a reward for your hard work?"

At this, Enrico couldn't help but break into a wide smile. "Okay!" he said. "You've got a deal!"

Carroll giggled at Enrico's excitement. The boy was a ball of energy—especially when he was excited—and they loved him for that. Drosselmeyer and Tanabata even stopped their fighting to watch Enrico bounce with joy. He was still bouncing when he and Drosselmeyer were waving the others goodbye.

"All right, Enrico," Drosselmeyer said once they

were alone, adding a mischievous wink. "Let's get in some practice!"

A little ways from the faeries' camp was a clearing in the woods stacked with wooden logs, pegs, and balls, all in the shapes to create new marionettes.

"All right," said Drosselmeyer as he walked around selecting a set of pieces. "Looks like Carroll asked the beavers to make some new parts for us after the 'incident' with my last puppet."

Enrico giggled. "Sorry, Drosselmeyer. I guess I got a little carried away."

Drosselmeyer chuckled. "I tease, but don't worry about it. We're happy you're getting so into it. You need to be able to protect yourself."

Yes, though the faeries did everything they could to keep Enrico out of harm's way, they also agreed that it couldn't hurt to teach the boy to fence—just in case. When he was old enough, they started him on his training regimen, Carroll enlisting the help of the beavers to make wooden marionettes and Drosselmeyer animating them to serve as sparring partners for Enrico. They taught him sport, and taught him defense, and always emphasized the harm in violence, balancing it with lessons on mindfulness, rest, and compassion.

Yet, their son loved to spar.

"All right," said Drosselmeyer as his creation sprung to life. "You've been doing well fighting basic puppets, even when I throw more than one at you. But what about a puppet with four arms?"

Enrico's eyes went wide at the sight of the wooden warrior before him, its four sturdy arms an imposing sight. "Four arms? But that's not fair!"

"Who said anything about it being fair?" said Drosselmeyer. "Do you think the soldiers are going to play fair if they're trying to capture you? You've got to be ready for anything."

"But, but," Enrico began, "there's no way I can beat that thing!"

Drosselmeyer smiled. "You said that the first time I had you go against three puppets at once. But you figured it out then, and you can figure it out now. Here. Use the padded swords so you don't get hurt. Are you ready?"

Enrico gave his opponent another once-over. Drosselmeyer was right, of course. Every new challenge he faced always seemed insurmountable at first, but that just made it all the more rewarding when he finally triumphed.

"All right!" Enrico cheered. "Game on!"

With that, the bout began. Drosselmeyer's latest creation was a formidable opponent. Enrico spared no effort attacking, dodging, and defending to the best of his abilities. But in spite of his determination, the marionette was too overwhelming, and with an unforeseen thrust, it knocked the boy to the ground.

"Enrico!" Drosselmeyer called out as he hurried over to the boy. "Are you okay?"

It took Enrico a moment to get back on his feet, but he was all smiles once he did. "Yeah, yeah, I'm fine. Come on. Let's go again. I'll get it this time."

Enrico did not get it the second time. The third time was not the charm either. Nor was the fourth or the fifth, and by his tenth loss, Drosselmeyer disengaged his powers and called it a day. Which wasn't to say either he or Enrico were disappointed with the day's training. For with every match,

Enrico came closer and closer to vanquishing his timbered adversary.

"Good hustle out there," Drosselmeyer said as Enrico plopped himself down in exhaustion.

"I'll get there," said Enrico, panting heavily. "I just need to keep trying."

"That's the spirit," said Drosselmeyer as he noticed Carroll and Tanabata approaching through the thickets.

"Hey!" Tanabata called out. "How was practice?"

"We had a good session today," said Drosselmeyer with a smile.

"Drosselmeyer had me duel against a puppet with four arms," Enrico said.

"Did he now?" said Carroll. "Well, it sounds like training is going well. Now then, how about we head back home, and we can put on that magic show I promised you?"

"All right!" Enrico cheered as he hopped back to his feet, and with that, the four of them made their way back to camp.

The faeries' magic shows never failed to amaze, and today was no exception.

"That was incredible!" Enrico cried with delight as the performance came to its conclusion. The faeries' hearts melted seeing their young boy bubbling over with excitement, and they couldn't help but laugh along with him.

"Tanabata?" he began after he had calmed down somewhat.

"Yes, Enrico?" said Tanabata.

"Can you make your lights into shapes? Like a bird? Or a flower? Or a star?"

"Make shapes? Well, I—"

"And Drosselmeyer!" Enrico interrupted. "What if you could make your puppets fall apart and come back together while they're dancing?"

"Huh, I guess I never—"

"Oh! Oh! And Carroll!" Enrico cried, hopping up and down. "What if you gave the animals something to play with in the show? Like juggling balls or twirling ribbons?"

"Slow down, slow down," Carroll giggled as she placed a hand on Encore's shoulder. "Enrico, you have so many good ideas, but we're still trying to master the tricks you came up with two weeks ago."

Enrico giggled. "I know, I know. It's just, I can picture all these great tricks in my head. I just want to see them!"

The faeries giggled some more as Enrico leapt away and spun around before landing gracefully on his back.

"Who knew there were so many different ways we could use our powers?" said Drosselmeyer.

"I know," said Tanabata. "I'd never even thought about making shapes with my lights before."

"Yes, our Enrico certainly has a flair for theatrics," said Carroll. "Which reminds me . . . Enrico, the three of us have a little gift for you."

"What is it?" Enrico asked.

"Well . . ." Carroll pulled a beautifully wrapped box from a hollowed-out tree stump. "Why don't you open it?"

"Thank you," Enrico said as he accepted the box from Carroll. He set it down gingerly and immediately got to work undoing the ribbon.

"Wow!" he gasped as he pulled out his present. It was a tall, ivory-colored top hat, much like one that a circus performer might wear. It was maybe a size or three too big for him and fell over his eyes when he tried to put it on, but that didn't bother Enrico.

"I love it!" he cried as he started hopping up and down again, much to his parents' amusement.

"Since you're always coming up with such creative ideas for how to use our powers, we thought it'd suit you," Carroll explained. "Now, if you'll hand me that ribbon over there, we'll see what we can do about having one of the birds learn to twirl it."

So were the days of Enrico's childhood, filled with fencing practice, magic shows, and playing in the woods, all the while remaining completely unaware of his true identity. Yet he never lost that spark of curiosity. As he grew older, he found himself longing more and more for something new and exciting. There came a point when fencing ceased to rouse his interest—where was the fun when he could slay five quad-wielding marionettes with minimal effort? And while he never tired of his parents' magic shows, they simply weren't enough to keep him entertained on their own. But he had promised he would stay hidden in the woods, and he very much wanted to honor his promise. And yet, he often found himself drawn to the edge of the forest—still hidden in the thickets—and from there he could see the human settlement of Corno Verde.

One day, when he was twelve years old, Enrico was looking longingly at the human town, beckoning him with its picturesque buildings and charming green hills, when he decided he could stand it no longer. He glanced around to make sure no one was nearby, then took off running.

Chapter 7:

The Renegade Mage
of Bellarossa

The settlement of Corno Verde was not a particularly bustling scene, but Enrico would never have guessed that from looking at it. Everywhere he turned, there was something new and exciting to him, and he could barely resist the urge to run around raving at the top of his lungs.

"Apples! Oranges! Peaches! One fiore each!" cried a produce vendor.

Baa! *Baa*! bleated a flock of sheep grazing under their shepherd's watchful eye.

Splash! *Splash*! went a water wheel as it was churned by a rushing stream.

Enrico was just ambling down the street, taking it all in, when he heard someone muttering and grunting with effort.

"Cursed wood chips! I can't wait until our cart is fixed!"

Enrico turned to see a boy who looked to be about his age. The stranger was carrying two large crates, and he was clearly having a difficult time of it. With a tremendous grunt, he set both crates down on the ground and sat on them to catch his breath.

"Hello," greeted Enrico. "Are you all right? Do you need some help?"

The boy looked up, panting heavily, and gave Enrico an appreciative smile. "Thank you, but I couldn't ask you for that. This stuff is heavy, and my place is still quite a long ways from here."

"It's no trouble, really," Enrico insisted.

The boy kept panting for a while, but eventually he gave a little nod. "Well . . . maybe I don't have a choice. There's no way I'm lugging these back home by myself. All right. If you're sure you don't mind. Thanks for the help. My name's Harvest, by the way."

"Enrico. Nice to meet you."

Harvest offered a smile and a hand, and Enrico accepted them both. After Harvest had

had another minute to rest, each boy took a crate, and off they went, following Harvest's lead.

"Thank you again," said Harvest as they were walking. "Normally, I'd load these into our horse cart, but old Cider hurt her hoof the other day. Nonno uses all these wood chips as mulch on the farm, in case you were wondering."

"He's a farmer?" said Enrico.

Harvest chuckled. "You're not from around here, are you? Everyone in Corno Verde knows Nonno Pumpkinseed. The fields you see to your left? All his. Nonno's farm is the largest in the province, and he shares the fruits of his labor with his fellow countryfolk on top of that. He must feed at least fifty people a week, I'll bet. Princess Gateau herself even came by once to give him a medal for his service. But you'll have a chance to meet him yourself soon enough. Here we are now!"

Sure enough, the boys had arrived at a rather handsome-looking farmhouse, with acres of fruit and vegetable fields stretching as far as the eye could see on either side. Some distance ahead of them, they saw an older gentleman approaching, but this was no ordinary man. He stood at just under seven feet in stature, with a broad, robust build, and behind him was a cart loaded with crates he was pulling along all by himself.

"Harvest," greeted the older man, his voice warm and resonant. "Perfect timing. I just got back from Signor Wheatley's with the fertilizer. Who's this?"

"Nonno, this is Enrico," said Harvest. "He was just helping me carry the wood chips back home."

"Enrico," said the old man. "Well, Enrico, I'm Nonno Pumpkinseed. Thank you for helping bring in the supplies. And thank you, Harvest. All right. I've got to get started spreading this fertilizer. Harvest, I'll leave our guest to you."

"We can help out with the crops," volunteered Harvest. "Oh, sorry Enrico, I didn't mean to—"

"No, no, it's fine," said Enrico with a smile. "I'd love to help out."

Harvest grinned. "I thought you would."

With that, Nonno Pumpkinseed led the way to the edge of the farm where a sea of tiny, green sprouts was just beginning to pop out of the soil. As the three of them were spreading the fertilizer, Enrico took a moment to take a great, deep breath and admire the glory of the vast, verdant acres around him.

"Nonno used to be the governor around these parts," explained Harvest, who had taken notice of Enrico's awestruck expression. "That's how we were able to buy all this farmland. Of course, that was a while ago. Before he resigned."

"Why did he resign?" asked Enrico.

"I'll tell you why," said Nonno Pumpkinseed without looking up. "I left because of Jean-Claude's tax hike. Three hundred fiori an adult. It's grand theft is what it is. I couldn't abide by it. No, not me. I'd have sooner given up my grandmother's pitchfork than enforce that loathsome tax and put my fellow countryfolk out on the streets."

Enrico nodded. "I see. Yeah, that makes sense. My parents complain about Jean-Claude all the time." He scratched his head. "They think I don't listen."

"They warn you for good reason, and you'd be better off to listen. And watch where you say such things. You're safe here, but you say that to the wrong snitch and they'll haul you off." He tapped his shovel against the ground.

"Oy, don't get Nonno started," chuckled Harvest.

"Too late," said Nonno Pumpkinseed. "Jean-Claude is a scoundrel, plain and simple. A disgrace to King Johannes and all of the other good kings before him."

"King Johannes was a good king, wasn't he?" said Enrico with a smile.

"A glorious king," said Nonno Pumpkinseed with a nostalgic sigh. "Always looking out for his people. I remember how he commissioned brigades of cooks to set up soup kitchens in every province of the kingdom during the Great Locust Blight. Not to mention all the hospitals and harbors and schoolhouses he ensured. And the people of Corno Verde still talk about the time when the Tempest's goons ransacked the town, and the good king waived the entire province's taxes for a year. Oh, what a wise and loving king. It was a pleasure to govern under him. But alas, he left us too soon. And with Jean-Claude. Bah! He's a fiend, all right. He's been nothing but a plague on the kingdom ever since he ascended the throne. Bellarossa must be weeping."

"You got that right!" said a boy's voice, and Enrico, Harvest, and Nonno Pumpkinseed turned to see two children—a boy and a girl the same age as Harvest and Enrico—standing by the fence gate.

"You bashing Jean-Claude again?" asked the girl with a smile.

"Nonno's really going at it this time," Harvest chuckled.

"Can't say I blame him," said the boy. "When we couldn't pay our taxes last season, the collectors took nearly half our chickens. You should have seen how mad my dad was."

"Yup," concurred the girl. "Same thing happened with my uncle's orchard. Heck, 1 doubt there's a single person in Corno Verde who's better off since Jean-Claude took the reins."

Harvest got up and walked over to the gate, beckoning Enrico to follow. "Omelette, Marmalade, this is Enrico. Enrico, meet Omelette and Marmalade. They're friends from town."

Greetings were exchanged, then Harvest said, "I'm heading out, Nonno. Can you take care of the rest of this yourself?"

"Don't worry about me," said Nonno Pumpkinseed with a wave. "Have fun."

With that, Harvest opened the gate. But before

he left, he turned to Enrico and said, "Hey, Enrico. You want to join us?"

"Um, are you sure?" Enrico asked, taken aback by the abrupt invitation.

"Sure, why not?" asked Harvest as the three children smiled at Enrico. "The people of Corno Verde take hospitality very seriously, you'll soon learn."

"Yeah, come on, Enrico," said Omelette.

"We would love to show you around town," said Marmalade.

Enrico felt himself flush. "O-okay. Thank you."

And with that, the four of them made their way to the plaza. And from the way they talked and laughed together, no one would have guessed that Enrico had not been a lifelong friend.

"Here, we should take Enrico to the park," suggested Marmalade. "There are always amazing street musicians there."

"Good idea," said Omelette. "But let's stop by Signora Almondine's bakery on the way. I'll bet there's a fresh batch of something or other being pulled from the ovens just about now."

"Sounds like a plan," said Harvest. "Come on, everyone. Let's go."

So passed the children their day of recreation, enjoying the best of what Corno Verde had to offer. From the spellbinding melodies of the street musicians to Signora Almondine's famous jam-filled cupcakes, Enrico savored it all. And when the time came for everyone to go their separate ways for the night, Harvest and Enrico bid the others goodbye and started the walk back to Harvest's.

"So, what did you think of town?" Harvest asked, a tired smile on his face.

"It was amazing," said Enrico, also with a smile. "Everyone seems really nice, and there's so much to see and do."

"Come back anytime," said Harvest. "We're always happy to have guests."

Enrico nodded. "Thank you, I will. Until next time."

The boys gave each other a little wave, and with that, Enrico started the long walk back to camp.

It was dark by the time he made it back. So dark in fact that he likely would have gotten lost in the woods had he not spent his whole life navigating them. When he arrived at camp, he was met with a trio of unhappy faeries.

"Where were you?" asked Drosselmeyer, gentle but firm.

"I'll tell you where he was," Tanabata huffed. "He was off in the human town. Weren't you?"

"Enrico, is this true?" asked Carroll, concern in her voice. "You know you're not supposed to go into town."

"Nothing . . . happened," said Enrico. From the looks on their faces, Enrico could tell that none of them were satisfied with his explanation.

"Enrico," Carroll began. "How many times do we have to tell you? It's for your own safety. You could get into serious trouble—"

"So could you!" said Enrico. "You have to cover up your wings every time you go into town, but you go anyway! Because you were right. People are amazing. They're kind and compassionate, and the stuff they make is just incredible! Please. Don't tell me I can't go back. I can't bear to stay away."

The three exchanged conflicted looks as they weighed their duty against their compassion. They excused themselves for a moment to confer amongst themselves, and when they came back, Carroll spoke first.

"Enrico, we talked it over, and have decided that *if* you can allow us to supervise you ... we can take you to town once a week and no more."

"We know the situation hasn't been fair to you," sighed Drosselmeyer. "You deserve to have normal experiences of a child your age, as many as we can offer."

"We're just worried about your safety, okay?" said Tanabata as she gingerly placed a hand on Enrico's shoulder. "Just ... promise us you'll be careful?"

Enrico smiled and embraced the ruby-winged Faerie. "I promise. Thank you so much for understanding."

Once the two of them broke apart, Enrico turned to see Carroll and Drosselmeyer smiling at them.

"All right," Carroll began. "If we're going to keep an eye on you, I think the best course of action would be to stay on your person at all times."

No sooner had she finished her words than Carroll and the other faeries began to shrink. Enrico watched with wide eyes as his three protectors grew smaller and smaller until they were no larger than mice. Then they flew into Enrico's tunic where they could remain unseen by anyone else.

"Hmm, we might want to sew some pockets in here before we head out next," Carroll squeaked. "We can take care of that in a day or two."

"Didn't remember we could shrink, did you?" tittered Drosselmeyer, and Enrico shook his head. "We used to do this trick for you when you were a baby, but you were never very impressed by it, so we stopped."

"But now, it's going to help us keep an eye on you," chirped Tanabata. "As long as you've got us with you, we'll keep you safe . . . just *please* try not to move around too much."

Enrico broke into a grin and gave a vigorous nod. "You've got it!"

And so, Enrico proceeded to make regular trips to Corno Verde. When Harvest was busy, Enrico was more than happy to help him and Nonno Pumpkinseed on the farm. When Harvest was free, Enrico would join him and his friends in celebrating festivals, attending Princess Lyric's concerts, or simply passing lazy afternoons in the town plaza. And the three faeries stayed with him all the while, shrunken down and hidden in the folds of his tunic.

One day, Harvest invited Enrico to help distribute Nonno's crops amongst the townsfolk as they did on a weekly basis. It was a festive scene—everyone cheering for their town hero—and the boys could feel themselves feeding off the crowd's good energy.

"Bless you, Nonno," said an older woman. "You're the hero of Corno Verde."

"I'll say!" said someone else. "I wish you were still in charge around these parts."

"Nonno Pumpkinseed for governor! No, Nonno Pumpkinseed for king!"

The townsfolk carried on in this manner, singing their hero's praises, and Nonno Pumpkinseed simply nodded in humble acceptance of their gratitude.

Then, without warning, the crowd went silent. It seemed they had an unexpected visitor, and the people parted to allow her to pass through.

"Admiral Allardyce," Harvest whispered to Enrico. "What is *she* doing here? It's not a tax day."

Nonno Pumpkinseed paid the admiral no mind as she sauntered up to him, her obsidian coat flowing behind her as she walked.

"Good day, Nonno," greeted the admiral with a tip of her magnificent tricorne.

"Admiral," said Nonno Pumpkinseed, not looking up from his task. "To what do I owe this visit?"

"Well," began the admiral with a fake and unpleasant smile. "It just so happens that some o' me soldiers overheard the locals singin' yer praises. And as I happened to be in the area, I just wanted to take the opportunity to meet such a model subject doin' his part to help his fellow countryfolk."

"Thank you, Admiral," said Nonno Pumpkinseed. "Well, if that's all, I wouldn't like to keep you."

"Well, actually, there is summat else," said the

admiral. "Ye see, the people are so very fond o' ye, Governor Scallion thought His Majesty the king ought to be informed. Now, the king be a good man, Nonno. He's worried about ye."

"Why? Has he made it illegal to feed the hungry?"

"Not at all," said the admiral. "No, he's merely worried that tending the farm might be gettin' to be too much for ye to handle in yer old age. Says that after yer years of service to the state, ye should be takin' it easy in yer retirement . . . and *not* breakin' yer back workin' the farm."

"Give Jean-Claude my thanks for his concern," said Nonno Pumpkinseed. "But I like what I do. You can tell him I have no intention of stopping anytime soon."

"It's King Jean-Claude to you." The admiral shrugged before giving another tip of her tricorne. "And I'll surely tell him. Suit yerself."

The crowd parted once more to allow the admiral to return to her carriage. But the air of anxiety she left behind lingered well past her departure. And as Enrico looked around to see all the faces that had been smiling just minutes ago now clouded with dread, he felt a profound sense of unwellness settle on his heart that stayed with him for the rest of the day.

"Enrico, are you all right?"

It was later that evening, and they were back at camp. Enrico turned to see Drosselmeyer looking up from the barrel of mead he was brewing. "You've been staring into the fire all night."

"He's upset about what happened earlier," Tanabata said.

"You want to talk about it?" offered Drosselmeyer. No response.

Drosselmeyer and Tanabata turned to Carroll, who was just as much at a loss as they were.

"Well," she sighed. "If he doesn't want to talk about it, we shouldn't force him. Let's just give him some space for now. Hopefully, he'll feel better in the morning."

But he didn't. In fact, he was every bit as upset when he got up as he had been the previous night. He spent the morning moping around camp, and it made the faeries' hearts feel heavy to see him that way. Finally, Carroll spoke up.

"Come on, Enrico," she said. "Let's go see your friends in town."

Enrico turned to look at Carroll in surprise. "Are you sure? But we just went yesterday."

"I know," said Carroll. "But there's no point in sitting around bored all day. It's fine. We know you'll be careful."

Drosselmeyer and Tanabata also gave their assent, and the light returned to Enrico's face. "Thanks, everyone," he said as he got back on his feet. And with that, the four of them were off to town.

"Enrico!" Harvest said when he saw his friend at his door. "Didn't expect to see you again so soon. Perfect timing. Come on in. There's something I want to show you."

Enrico followed Harvest into the parlor where Nonno Pumpkinseed was standing over an enormous deer carcass.

"Found him this morning devouring our lettuce like he was starved," said Harvest. "I wasn't sure what to do, but people need our food. Can you believe how big it is?"

"It's a behemoth, all right," said Nonno Pumpkinseed. "I didn't think an animal could just smash through my fence like that. Harvest, I'm glad you killed it, and quickly before it could do *too* much damage. And now we've got venison to make up for what was lost."

"Join us for dinner, Enrico?" Harvest offered. "There's plenty for us and the villagers too."

"I'd like that," Enrico said with a smile. And with that, the three of them got to work cleaning the carcass in preparation for the night's meal.

Later that night, the three of them sat down to a feast. Thick cuts of hearty venison, pinkish red in the center, dark brown on the outside. Mashed potatoes—light and fluffy—and a medley of roasted fall vegetables. Add to that fresh garden salad and rolls and cheese and butter, and Encore very nearly feared that he might just swallow the whole table, silverware and all.

"What a spread," cheered Harvest. "Too bad Omelette and Marmalade are both out of town. We're eating like kings tonight."

"Remember your gratitude," said Nonno Pumpkinseed. "Not many people can afford to eat like this."

"I know, I know," said Harvest. "That's the whole reason we give away our crops, after all."

"Speaking of which," Enrico began. "What do you think about what the admiral was saying the other day? Are you worried?"

Nonno Pumpkinseed snorted. "No. If she thinks she can scare me from feeding the hungry, she's got another thing coming. I'll be out there distributing food again next week. Same time. Same place. Just like always."

"You're welcome to join us, Enrico," said Harvest through a mouthful of potatoes. "It's always fun having you around."

Enrico couldn't help but smile at his companions' unwavering resolve. "Count me in. I'm always happy to help."

And so he did. The next week, Nonno Pumpkinseed and Harvest were out distributing crops, same as usual, with Enrico there to help out. The unpleasantness of last week seemed but a distant memory, and the townsfolk were as festive as ever. But just like the previous week, that all changed once Admiral Allardyce arrived on the scene.

"Good day, Nonno," she greeted in her sea-salted voice.

"Admiral," said Nonno Pumpkinseed. "What brings you here today?"

"Well, Nonno, perhaps ye can tell me," said the admiral as she flashed a wicked grin. "Upstandin' subject that ye are, I could hardly believe me ears when I heard the news."

"What are you talking about?" asked Nonno Pumpkinseed.

"Well, ye see," the admiral began. "Only earlier this week, the palace ranchers reported that one o' the king's deer had gone missin' and was seen running off towards Corno Verde. So o' course, I dispatched a team o' soldiers to recover the lost animal. Only when they arrived, the beast was nowhere to be found. But eyewitnesses testified that it was last seen on yer estate. What's more, they said they witnessed the deer being shot down, and we've gone and recovered a hoof, marked with the king's ownership. Now, surely that can't be, Nonno? Surely ye must know that the penalty for poachin' the king's deer be life in the dungeon?"

At this, Nonno Pumpkinseed could only stare

at the admiral as realization sunk in. By his side, Harvest's eyes had gone wide.

"Wait, no wait," Harvest began. "You can't take him in! I was the one who—"

"Yes, I shot the deer," said Nonno Pumpkinseed. "No need to make a scene now. I'll come quietly."

With that, two soldiers advanced on Nonno Pumpkinseed with a pair of handcuffs as the crowd reacted with horror.

"No!" Harvest shrieked. "You can't take Nonno away!"

"Harvest, no!" Nonno Pumpkinseed said. "We can't fight this here. I'll work to find another way."

"Listen to your Nonno, brat," said Admiral Allardyce. "It's trouble enough dealin' with criminals without unruly pups gettin' in the way."

"Harvest, please," said Nonno Pumpkinseed. "You have to listen to me. I know it's terrible, but if you don't let me go, they might take you too."

"But, but," Harvest choked. "Nonno, the people need you. How am I ever going to take care of the farm without you?"

"Don't worry about the farm," said Nonno Pumpkinseed. "As long as you're okay, that's all that matters."

And though the boy was still distraught, he gave Nonno a silent nod.

The admiral coughed. "Well, not to break up such a tender moment, but we've several other matters to tend to, and we'd best be gettin' on our way."

With that, Nonno Pumpkinseed was hauled off, leaving Harvest and Enrico to process what had happened.

"Darn it!" Harvest wailed. "Nonno *thought* it was weird that a deer could break through the fences! And I didn't know why he was so hungry, why he wouldn't stop. Ugh! Rotten admiral!"

Enrico tried to console his friend but was unable to find the words. Instead, he simply sat by Harvest's side and kept him company as he let out his frustrations. And as Enrico looked at his friend, dejected and forlorn, he felt something well up in his chest. It was more than just anger. Revulsion, loathing, and indignation also weren't quite right. No, it was some noxious amalgamation of all of those mixed together with one or two other things thrown in. All induced by the wanton abuse that the admiral so casually inflicted on the people. And the pestilence festered restlessly in his chest well into the night.

Enrico was still seething that evening, back at camp.

"It's not right," he fumed. "How could a so-called king lock up a man just for feeding the hungry? It's tyranny is what it is. And there's no end in sight. I wish there was anything I could do."

For a while, the faeries simply watched in silence as Enrico seethed. Finally, Tanabata spoke.

"This is painful to watch."

"Yeah . . ." sighed Drosselmeyer. "We . . . we have to tell him, don't we?"

"I suppose you're right," conceded Carroll with a sigh. "Drosselmeyer, Tanabata, would you each be a dear and retrieve the stuff?"

The two nodded and flew high into the treetops.

Enrico looked at Carroll in confusion as she unhooked something metal from her own waist and sat down beside him, her expression warm but solemn. When the others returned, Tanabata was holding a golden crown, and Drosselmeyer had a message in a bottle. Carroll waited for them to sit down before she began to speak.

"Enrico, there's something we need to tell you. Something we probably should have told you a long time ago, and I'm sorry it took us so long. I just hope you're not *too* upset with us."

Enrico nodded but said nothing, his face still colored with confusion.

"Enrico is not the name of your birth. And your original parents weren't captured. No, your parents . . . your parents were the late King Johannes and Queen Soiree. You are the long lost Prince Encore. After your father's mysterious death, the court decided to send you overseas until you came of age, for your own safety. But your fleet never made it. You were attacked by pirates and washed up ashore where we found you along with your father's Admiral of the Navy, who explained the situation to us and entrusted us with your care, before his wounds took him. This, this was his signature chain, commissioned by your father upon his induction. He cared for you as family, and we wanted to save something of his for you."

As Carroll held out a thick metal chain with a distinctly stamped emblem, Encore's eyes grew wide with realization.

"Here," said Tanabata as she handed Encore

a finely wrought gold crown. "Your crown, when you're of age. The admiral gave us this to prove your identity as the prince when we brought you back."

"And your sisters wrote this letter for you," said Drosselmeyer as he handed him the bottle.

Encore didn't waste a second uncorking the bottle and reading the letter. He read it silently to himself, taking his time so as not to miss a word, and when he was done, he set it aside and brought his hands together in front of his face, deep in thought.

"We know that this must be a lot to take in," Carroll said as she gave Encore a sympathetic look. "Please, Enrico—er, Encore, if you'd like— you have to understand, when we took you under our care, we thought raising you was going to be so much fun—"

"And it was. Don't get us wrong," Drosselmeyer interjected.

Carroll nodded in agreement. "But the truth is, well, we didn't really know what we were getting ourselves into. We thought you would be safer not knowing, but we didn't think how it might impact you when you learned the truth. And that was our mistake.”

“We just hope you’re okay,” Tanabata said.

The prince nodded in understanding. At first, he didn’t say a word, but after a few moments, he found his voice again.

“I’d like to go by Encore. You gave me a beautiful name, but Encore feels right, somehow. And . . . I’m not upset,” he said. “I know you were trying your best.”

“Are you sure?” asked Carroll. “You don’t have to spare our feelings.”

“No, really,” said Encore as he gave them a smile. “I’ll be okay.”

Drosselmeyer smiled. “We’re so glad to hear you say that.”

“We never meant for you to get hurt,” said Tanabata as she leaned in for a hug.

“You know, Encore. We faeries have a saying, born of centuries living as outcasts and drifters.”

“Family is heart, not blood,” the three faeries murmured together.

“So, if you’ll still have us . . . In whatever way you . . .”

“You are the only parents I still have,” Encore

said, his voice wavering, reaching to hug Tanabata back, Carroll and Drosselmeyer joining them promptly. They stayed like that for a while, and when they broke up, Encore's smile was as bright as ever.

"Actually, this is amazing news," he said. "If Prince Encore—that means me—is alive, then the line was never properly passed."

"We still have to wait five more years before we can bring you back," cautioned Drosselmeyer. "You'd be far too vulnerable if you went back now."

"Well, I can't just sit around and do nothing while the kingdom suffers," said Encore. "I have a responsibility to my people. To my friends."

"I was afraid you might say that," sighed Carroll. But the unease quickly left her face, replaced by a faint smile and a twinkle in her eyes. Drosselmeyer and Tanabata were smiling as well. "All right, but we're not letting you go alone."

The sign above the door for the next room read: MELODY CARAMELS. In the center of the room was an enormous oven with a great funnel on top, and from its center came a strange, enchanting sort of music, as if a symphony were being baked within. Two grand staircases led up to the funnel, and at the top of the stairs, gnomes were busy feeding it bucketfuls of violet fruit. There was a pipe coming out of the front of the oven, and every few seconds, a golden caramel would pop out. At the door of the oven, there were more gnomes dumping in shovelfuls of glitter, and each time they did, the flames would dance to the swell of the music, mesmerizing Ike.

"This here is my latest creation," announced the Gumdrop Faerie. "I call them melody caramels. Those violet fruits you see going into the funnel are a very peculiar kind of fruit indeed. They're called symphony berries, and when they're exposed to extreme heat, they release a special kind of juice that makes for the most marvelous candies. Look! Over there, see!"

She gestured towards a trio of gnomes who were sampling some fresh melody caramels. They each popped one of the little candies into their mouths, and a few seconds later, they began to whistle. But the sounds that escaped their mouths sounded nothing like ordinary whistling. Rather, their tones sounded exactly like those of musical instruments—crisp and clear—one in trumpet, one in flute, and one in piano.

"Aren't they amazing?" said the Gumdrop Faerie. "And if you eat a whole bunch of them, it's like having a whole orchestra in your mouth. Although the sound could be a bit clearer. You see, the stronger the fire, the more juice the berries produce. Keeping the flames stoked with magic glitter at all times is quite important."

At this, Ike could barely contain himself. "Gumdrop Faerie!" he exclaimed. "Please, oh please, let me help the gnomes tend the fire!" He looked up, worried, as adults often scolded his distraction.

The Gumdrop Faerie only giggled. "Look, they

are bringing you your own boy-size shovel. Go on, then."

A gnome came up to present Ike with a shovel, and just like that, he was off like a flash, hurrying about shoveling glitter into the oven to make the flames do their dance for him. Sometimes from one color, sometimes another, the gnomes didn't seem to mind.

The Gumdrop Faerie smiled as she watched the boy zip around. After a while, she excused herself and made her way back to the confectionery's front room where she passed the time until, just before supper bell, the gnomes brought the children back to her.

"Did you all enjoy your tour of the shop?" she asked, smiling at the children.

"Oh yes!" they exclaimed. "It was wonderful!"

"I'm very glad to hear that," giggled the Gumdrop Faerie. "You're all welcome to come back and help out again whenever you like."

At this, the children's eyes widened, and sparkled with delight.

"You don't really mean it?" they cried.

"I do indeed," said the Gumdrop Faerie. "Each and every one of you was so helpful today, I would love to have you back again. I'll even show you more rooms if you like. As for tonight, why don't you each make a complimentary basket of treats to take home with you?"

Now the children shimmered with excitement.

"Thank you! Thank you! Thank you!" they cried to the Faerie and each of the smiling gnomes. "We'll come by to help whenever we can!"

The Gumdrop Faerie smiled as the children filled their baskets and hurried home. All of the children came back to the confectionery the next day. And the day after that. And the day after that.

Ike was good at shoveling glitter, and he talked with the gnomes every day about new ways he could find focus when he wanted to, and how to be happy being himself. Nevi loved to gather eggs, and had started to dress more like a gnome, their smile now nearly glittering like the glitter of the eggs they collected. Amber no longer painted alone, but with the other gnomes, who didn't comment at all on her tics, and always loved to be in her company. And Julius, he still talked the least of the group, but he was no longer nervous joining in when he had something he wanted to add, for the fruit-mashing team had shown him that he could be himself around friends, that true friends didn't worry if he sometimes didn't know how to say things the way others did.

The children made delicious sweets for everyone to enjoy, as they became friends with gnomes and other children alike. And before long, they became the Gumdrop Faerie's fully fledged apprentices in candy making.

"We love you, Gumdrop Faerie!" the children said with a hug each time they left the shop for the day.

And the Gumdrop Faerie simply smiled in return and said, "I love you too."

Chapter 8:

The Royal Family
of Bellarossa

Encore finished recounting his tale, and the princesses took a moment to process his story.

"Well," Alex began, "I must commend you. You certainly have done your part to take care of the kingdom."

The prince flashed a smile.

"However," she continued, "as long as Jean-Claude sits on the throne, the people will continue to suffer. And something tells me he isn't just going to surrender the crown if you come strolling into the palace."

At this, the prince frowned. "I know. I know," he sighed. "I won't rest as long as Nonno is in that dungeon, or anyone else is being hurt by that fiend. I've been trying every day to think of a way to get rid of Jean-Claude myself, but so far, I've got nothing."

The princesses drooped, as if visibly burdened by the prospect of suffering through more of Jean-Claude's regime.

"Ah, well," said the prince, forcing a smile. "I'm sure we'll figure something out. In the meantime, how would you all like to meet the faeries?"

No sooner had the word left his mouth than three figures—no larger than mice—darted out of the folds of Encore's tunic. They shot about ten feet into the air and grew in size until they were nearly as big as the princesses before they made their descent. They looked to be around twenty years old, with wings that shimmered like gemstones in the moonlight. And as the princesses admired their new visitors, each of them thought that they had never seen such exquisite beauty.

"Your wings look like stained glass!" Palette cried.

"And the styling of your hair! Gorgeous!" gushed Alamode.

"I can't believe it," Gateau whispered. "Real faeries . . ."

"Wow, just . . . what a wonderful world." Lyric sighed.

"So the legends are true," mused Alex.

The faeries smiled at the princesses' reactions of excitement and delight and gave them a moment to take it all in.

"All right, then," Encore began once everyone had calmed down somewhat. "Who wants to introduce themself first?"

"Me! Me!" insisted the ruby-winged faerie. "Hi, everyone! I'm Tanabata! I can conjure up dancing lights. Watch!" And with that, she began to recite an incantation.

Star light, star bright, little star of mine
Gleam and glow! There you go! Shine! Shine! Shine!

As she chanted, Tanabata's wings sparkled with fiery, ruby light. With a snap of her fingers, a flurry of colored lights erupted around her, sending each of the princesses a few steps back in surprise.

"Whoa! Whoa! Come on, Tanabata! Don't startle them!" laughed the sapphire-winged faerie. He smiled as Tanabata concluded her exhibition, then said, "Nice to meet you! I'm Drosselmeyer. I can animate puppets and make them dance and play."

Right on cue, Encore withdrew three figurines from his satchel and tossed them in Drosselmeyer's direction. The grinning faerie waved his hands at them and said:

Empty vessels, cast away
Come to life, it's time to play!

Drosselmeyer's wings glistened with vibrant, sapphire light, and the toy figurines came to life. They landed gracefully on their feet before launching into a little acrobatics routine, and after they finished, one of the figurines approached Alex to offer her a kiss on the hand.

"I suppose that leaves me," said the emerald-winged Faerie. "Hello, Your Majesties. My name is Carroll. I can talk to animals. Please, allow me to demonstrate." She brought her hands to her heart and said:

Hear me, every beast and bird
Come to me and heed my word.

Carroll's wings gleamed with warm, emerald light, and before long, a bird came to perch on Carroll's hand, a squirrel and a couple of rabbits running up to her feet shortly after. Carroll giggled. "Well, I imagine most of the animals are asleep right now, but you get the idea."

The princesses were even more impressed than they had already been. Each of them marveled in sheer delight at the very real magic, and Alex's inquisitive mind was already racing as she tried to make sense of what she had just witnessed. She took a moment to collect herself, then addressed the faeries.

"Thank you very much for taking care of my brother all these years," she said, her sisters following her lead and giving their thanks as well.

"Please, think nothing of it," said Carroll. "It was an absolute pleasure to take care of the prince."

Encore's head rose, in sudden thought. "They're my family, too. And you're my family. So, then, they could be your family, too."

He glanced nervously at the three, who exchanged their own glances. Carroll spoke. "We'd love that."

Alex's heart rose at the thought, but she wasn't fully ready to consider it. Perhaps it was her affinity for story, but questions were springing to mind. "Please, forgive me for being so bold, but I must confess to great curiosity as to how your powers work."

The faeries giggled amongst themselves before Carroll said, "Of course. It's only natural that you should be curious. Go ahead. Ask us anything you like."

"Thank you," said Alex. She took a brief pause before starting. "Well, if you have the power to talk to animals, does that mean you can command them as well?"

"Well, not quite," said Carroll thoughtfully. "That is, I can talk with them, but I would not order them, only seek to persuade. And more aggressive animals like wolves and bears tend not to be very open to persuasion. Nor are animals accustomed to servitude—the royal cavalry, for instance. But your common woodland critter or domestic animal tends to be much more agreeable, and once you've earned their favor, they like to help."

"Fascinating," Alex murmured.

"How about me?" volunteered Tanabata. "Any questions about my dancing lights?"

Alex turned to Tanabata and thought for a moment before she noticed something. "Your lights . . . they look a lot like flames. Yet I notice the grass around you doesn't look to be burnt in the slightest."

"That's right," said Tanabata. "They may look like fire, but my lights are gentle. You could light up the whole forest with them and not hurt a fly."

"Okay, so they're safe around people, and indoors too. Good to know ..." mused Alex. Finally, she turned to Drosselmeyer. "In your case, I'm wondering what features a puppet needs in order for you to be able to animate it."

Drosselmeyer turned his gaze upwards as he considered Alex's question. "Well ... I suppose I can enchant anything as long as it has pieces it can understand to move. Can't get much out of a block of wood, for instance. But other than that, I can animate armor, scarecrows, dolls—"

"Statues?" asked Alex. "Could you animate a statue?"

"Yes, I'm pretty sure I could animate a statue," said Drosselmeyer.

"Interesting, interesting ..." Alex said. From the look on her face, her sisters could tell that the gears in her head were turning.

"What's on your mind, Alex?" asked Lyric.

"Hmm?" said Alex. "Well, I'm trying to think

of a plan to get rid of Jean-Claude that won't take five years. Let's see, with the tools at our disposal . . ."

Everyone gave Alex a minute or two to think before she heaved a great sigh of frustration, letting them know that even her brilliant mind was stumped.

"That wretched Jean-Claude," Palette muttered. "I can't bear to see him lay waste to our precious kingdom for another day. Mommy and Daddy would be so sad."

At this point, everyone noticed Encore wince.

"Are you okay?" Palette asked, noticing his discomfort. "Did I say something?"

"Oh, no, no, it's nothing really," said Encore.

"No, please, you seem upset," Palette insisted.

"Oh," said Encore. "Well, it's just . . . you mentioned Mom and Dad. And, well, it just made me think about . . . about how I never got to meet our parents," he said with his eyes to the ground.

"Oh," said Palette as she flushed. "Oh no, I'm so sorry. Please, I didn't mean to make you feel bad. I don't really remember them either; I was too young. But, with my sisters' stories, I feel like I did. Oh, now, now I'm making it worse."

"No, no," Encore said. "Please, don't feel bad. It's okay, really . . . but, if I'm being honest, there were a lot of times—even before I knew who they were—when I used to lie awake at night, wishing that I could have met them or—I don't know—even heard their voices just once."

"Oh!" exclaimed Palette. "Well, there's one you can. Alex can do a perfect impression of Daddy. Show him, Alex!"

Encore turned to Alex. "Does it really sound just like him?"

"Oh, yes!" the princesses cried. "It's absolutely perfect! She used to be able to fool everyone, and when we were younger, we used it to joke and play!"

At this, Alex raised her eyebrows with mild surprise. She wasn't expecting to be put on the spot like that, but she didn't particularly mind. "Ah . . . yes, well, I suppose I could do my impression of Daddy."

It took Alex a moment to figure out what she wanted to say before it came to her. Without a word, she walked up to Encore and took his hands in her own before starting.

"Dearest son, how are you? I'm terribly sorry

your mother and I can't be with you right now. If you ever feel sad or lonely, please know that you have always been in our hearts. We're so proud of you for being so very brave and for staying noble and true no matter what challenges you faced. May you find a world full of magic."

When Alex was finished, tears were streaming down Encore's cheeks, and Alex spread her arms to welcome him into a hug, their sisters piling on immediately.

"Thank you," Encore whispered. "That was Dad's voice all right. I could tell."

"Her impression is spot on," Alamode said. "You actually cannot tell the difference."

"Yeah . . ." Alex said. Then a thought dawned on her, and she split from the group. "You're right . . . no one *can* tell the difference. Hmm . . . yes, I . . . I think I've got it now. We can't get any wolves . . . but maybe some of the palace dogs . . . and Palette could . . . yes, and Alamode could . . . yes! Yes! I've got it!"

"Got what?" asked a bewildered Gateau.

Alex beamed. "A plan to reclaim our kingdom. Everybody, listen up!"

The very next day, King Jean-Claude was passing through the corridors when he caught whiff of a most appetizing aroma. The scent was so disarming, the king couldn't help but stop in his tracks and breathe it in. And as he did, his mind flooded with memories of crackling fireplaces on frosty, winter evenings; of sumptuous banquets and beautifully wrapped presents; of cozy afternoons spent napping in bed; and of solitary strolls through neatly manicured rose gardens. As the king took in great, deep breaths of the delectable fragrance, he tried to think where he remembered it from. It was familiar, but he couldn't quite place his finger on it. Then it hit him. It was starberry tarts, the late king's favorite. Suddenly, the delicious aroma became nauseating, and the king bolted straight for the kitchen.

"Who's making starberry tarts?" he demanded as he burst through the doors. "I thought I ordered you never to make them again!"

The royal chefs just exchanged confused looks at the king's outburst.

"I'm sorry, Your Majesty, but we've not made starberry tarts since your order," the head chef informed him.

"That's absurd," retorted King Jean-Claude. "Come into the hall with me, and tell me you don't smell it."

The head chef followed the king into the corridor and agreed that there was no mistaking the signature scent of spiced, oven-baked starberry jam. "Yes, I do smell them. But I promise you we've not prepared them."

"Then where is that smell coming from?" demanded the king, unable to conceal his irritation.

"Who knows?" said the chef. "Maybe it's the ghost of the late king."

The chef chuckled at his own joke as King Jean-Claude felt a shiver go down his spine.

"Get back to work," he muttered.

The chef shrugged and returned to the kitchen. Neither of them noticed the shrunken-down faeries that had been eavesdropping on their conversation just outside the window. Once the king left the hallway, the three flew off, making their way towards the north tower.

At the north tower, the windows to Gateau's kitchen were open, and three faeries flew in to find Alex, Gateau, and Encore gathered around the ovens.

"You were right, Alex!" exclaimed Tanabata. "Jean-Claude was totally spooked!"

"Good call making the tarts here," chuckled Drosselmeyer. "I don't think it even crossed his mind that the scent could be coming all the way from the tower."

"Well, it's all thanks to your magic really," said Gateau as she removed a fresh batch of starberry tarts from the oven. "If it weren't for you enchanting my oven and utensils, these wouldn't have turned out nearly as nice."

"Hey," said Alex. "Give yourself some credit. Your baking is amazing."

"I'll say. These are incredible, Sis," said Encore, his speech muffled by a mouthful of tart.

"Ah, no . . ." Gateau began as her face went red.

"Gateau," said Carroll. "I don't think you understand. We might be able to enchant your tools, but it's still up to you to make the most of them. This wonderful fragrance wouldn't be possible if you weren't already such a talented chef. All we did was bring it out a little more."

"Listen to her, Sis," said Alex with a smile. "You should be proud of yourself."

But in spite of their encouraging words, Gateau remained unconvinced.

"All right, you know what? Enough of this," Alex said. "I'm not messing around anymore. Here's what we're going to do. You're going to try one of your tarts—right here, right now—and if you can look me in the eye and tell me it's not delicious, I'll let this whole thing go. But if not, you have to admit what an amazing chef you are, okay?"

"Alex—" Gateau began.

"No, no, no," Alex cut her off. "Come on, Gateau. Just try one."

Gateau hesitated for a moment, but at Alex's urging, she picked up a tart off the tray and took a timid little bite. Starberry tarts were an exceptionally difficult dish to master. The berries themselves were notoriously prone to overcaramelization and required just the right balance of sugar and spice so as not to overpower the fruit's rich yet subtle flavor, or nullify its perfectly tantalizing scent. But Gateau's tarts were absolutely perfect, and the princess of cuisine couldn't help but crack a smile as her mouth filled with the immaculate taste of an expertly prepared starberry tart.

"Well?" asked Alex as she saw Gateau's face light up. "How is it?"

"It's good," Gateau said with a faint, little smile. "Really good."

"She says it's good!" Encore whooped as he threw up his hands in triumph.

The siblings and faeries giggled before Alex said, "See? I told you so. Your cooking is amazing, Gateau. That's why I'm trusting you with this part of the plan. You know I wouldn't have asked you if I didn't think you were up to the task."

Gateau let out a great breath, and her smile grew even brighter. "I know, thanks for believing in me, Sis." She took another moment to collect herself. "Speaking of the plan, you might want to go check on Palette and Alamode. See how they're doing."

"Good idea," said Alex. With that, she excused herself to head over to Palette's studio. The princesses of paint and cloth were so engrossed in their work, they didn't even hear her open the door.

"This look like the right shade to you?" Palette asked Alamode as she held out a sample.

"Little more blue. The coat was Lafetian mink dyed with the finest indigo in Corona Regis. It needs to be richer than that," said Alamode. "And maybe add just the *tiniest* hint of color to the lining? Even winter ermine isn't going to look *that* white when it gets to be that old."

"Yeah, you're right," said Palette. "All right. Cool. I'll get to work on that."

"Hey, you two. How's it going?"

The princesses turned to see their older sister standing behind them.

"Alex!" said Palette. "I'll have to thank the faeries again for enchanting my brushes and paints for me. I'm painting like I've never painted before, and it feels incredible! Oh, and I can't forget to give Alamode credit too. Even with my eye for color, having an expert like her is going to go a long way in making this look as realistic as possible."

Alamode beamed. "Thanks, Pally. I have to say, it really is something else watching you work like this. I'll have to ask the faeries to enchant my fabric and sewing needles later."

"Glad to hear it," said Alex with a nod. "Do you think it'll be ready in time?"

"Oh yeah," said Palette, brimming with confidence. "Yeah, it'll be ready. You can count on us."

In spite of her nerves, Alex couldn't help but crack a slight grin. Everything was going according to plan. Lyric was up next. Then it was time for the grand finale.

The following evening, down in the courtyard, people were going about their usual business when all of a sudden, they heard a hauntingly beautiful melody coming from nowhere. Though no lyrics accompanied the music, there was no mistaking the tune. And many present couldn't help themselves but sing along.

O great King Johannes, know you are in our hearts
We know that you are with us, though you had to
depart . . .

As the first verse concluded, people started to snap out of their trance and talk amongst themselves.

"Where is it coming from?" asked someone.

"Who cares? It's absolutely beautiful!" said another voice.

"Oh, the late king's spirit must be watching over us," said someone else.

Though the music was mollifying to most in the courtyard, one individual was less than impressed. King Jean-Claude, who had been feeling frazzled ever since the Harvest Jamboree.

"Who's playing that music?" he barked. His outburst drew the attention of everyone in the courtyard, and the king felt himself wilt under their gaze. "Please, pardon me," he mumbled. "I haven't been feeling quite well. Please, forget what just happened, and carry on."

Meanwhile on Lyric's balcony, the princess of song brought her tune to its conclusion and her flute from her lips as Alex watched from her seat on a bench.

"That was beautiful," said Alex.

"Thanks," said Lyric with a smile as she sat down next to Alex. "That really was something. Playing an enchanted flute. I don't think I've ever sounded so good. I just wish Encore weren't busy rehearsing for tomorrow. As a fellow performer, I would have loved to play for him."

"Yeah," said Alex. "But you'll have plenty of time to share your art with each other after tomorrow. At least I hope so."

Lyric chuckled. "Feeling nervous, are we?"

"Maybe just a bit," Alex admitted. "Are you?"

"Well," Lyric began. "There's no denying that the stakes are high. But none of us are in this alone. You know you can always lean on me when you're not strong. So lay your weary head to rest. I got a feeling that every little thing is going to be all right."

Alex smiled as she took in her sister's words. "Thanks, Sis. I hope so."

At the door to her own suite, Alex placed a hand on the doorknob when she had an idea. After a moment's pause, she entered her suite, grabbed a lantern, and descended the tower.

It wasn't long before she arrived at her destination, the Faerie Well, which was every bit as decrepit as it had been the other day. But unlike then, Alex didn't find herself unsettled by the well's run-down state. No, not tonight. Tonight, as she regarded the monument before her, she felt a strange sort of peace.

"Oh, hey," said a voice, pulling Alex out of her thoughts. The princess turned around to see Encore standing a little ways behind her. "Didn't expect to see you here. I just got back from practice."

"Did you now?" Alex asked as Encore walked up beside her. "Well, how did it go?"

"It went well," Encore chuckled. "I think we've really got the routine down. You should have seen Tanabata's lights. Jean-Claude is in for a real shock."

Alex chuckled at her little brother's words. "Good, good. I'm glad to hear it."

And with that, the conversation was over.

For the siblings didn't need any more words. As brother and sister stood side by side in companionable silence, beholding the run-down Faerie Well, each of them knew what the other was thinking.

The nightmare will be over soon.

The following morning, the Corona siblings and the faeries were gathered in a storage room while Alamode kept watch over the courtyard.

"So we all know what we're doing, right?" Alex asked one last time.

"We passed on the message," said Lyric. "Court ministers and navy officers should be gathering outside the throne room any minute."

"All right!" Encore cheered as he pumped his fists. "Let's take back our kingdom!"

Suddenly, the doors flew open, and in came Alamode.

"Everyone," she said. "Admiral Allardyce is headed for the throne room. What should we do?"

Alex turned to the faeries. "Do you think you can listen in on their conversation?"

"Of course," they said as they shrank down before flying over to the throne room. They slipped in undetected when the guards opened the doors and ducked into a potted plant where they could listen without being seen.

"Admiral," began King Jean-Claude. His expression and tone were weary. "There's something I've been meaning to talk to you about. It's been on my mind since the Harvest Jamboree."

"Aye, Yer Majesty?" said the admiral.

"Well, it's about the Renegade Mage . . ." the king began before trailing off.

"Aye?" said the admiral, prompting the king to go on.

"Yes, well, it occurs to me . . . he's about the same age that the prince would be if he were alive today, isn't he?"

"Yer Majesty," said the admiral. "The prince be dead. I give ye me oath on me honor as a pirate. Those were the terms of our agreement, and the Tempest always makes good on her word."

"Yes, yes," said the king with a dismissive wave. "You off the prince at sea so I can take the throne, and I appoint you my Admiral of the Navy so you can retire from a life of piracy and enjoy a cut of the tax revenue. And yet . . . one can't help but notice . . . notice how he has the late king's eyes. His hair too. And surely, you see the lilt of his mother's irritating smile."

"Yer Majesty, I assure you, the prince be naught but a ghost," the admiral insisted.

King Jean-Claude let out a great breath, then said, "Yes, yes. I suppose . . . and yet, learned though I may be, I find myself believing in ghost stories as of late. On that note, there's something else I'd like to discuss with you, Admiral."

"Aye, Yer Majesty?" said the admiral.

"Well, you see," began the king. "The Harvest Jamboree was the first time I saw the Mage with my own two eyes. And his powers, well . . . do they remind you of anything, Admiral?"

"Aye," she said. "The lad's witchin' be the same as that o' the Faeries o' lore. Just like the soldiers have been saying."

"Indeed," said the king. "It seems as though the Fae folk are here in Bellarossa. And it leads me to wonder . . . wonder if the aromas and the music from nowhere were their doing as well. It would make sense, considering it, for the Faeries to align with the old regime. King Johannes was a well-known patron of theirs, after all. In any case, if the legends are true, and the Faeries are here in Bellarossa, they could pose a threat to my reign."

"Aye, Yer Majesty," said the admiral. "What do ye propose we do about it?"

"Well," the king began. "The Faeries may have their witchcraft, but we have technological superiority. Blades, firearms, explosives. According to the legends, this is how we destroyed the Faeries' civilization in the woods and sent them into hiding all those centuries ago. I see no reason we couldn't do the same now. So Admiral, I want you to take your soldiers—as many as you can—and comb the forests, the shores, the mountains. Exterminate every last faerie you find, and bring them to me. I'll pay a hundred narcisi bounty for each pair of wings you procure."

At this, the admiral flashed a wicked grin. "Aye, aye, Yer Majesty, it shall be done," she said, and with a tip of her tricorne, she started for the door.

The faeries were horrified by what they had heard. They snuck out the doors as the admiral made her exit, then darted back to the storage room.

"Everyone!" Tanabata cried. "It's terrible! Absolutely terrible!"

"What is it?" asked Alex. "What happened in there?"

"Allardyce never defeated the Tempest; she is the Tempest! Jean-Claude asked her to exterminate the Faeries!" Tanabata cried. "They say they're going to send soldiers to hunt them down and massacre them all! Never again," she shouted, Drosselmeyer and Carroll moving over to each place a hand on her shoulders.

The princesses murmured in shock. "We can never let that happen!"

But none of the siblings was more affected by the news than Encore.

"So she was the one who tried to end me that night?" he fumed. "She killed all those trying to protect me? And now she thinks she's going to hunt down the Faeries? She won't touch my family again." He turned to his siblings. "Everyone, you don't need me right now. If I'm not back in time, the faeries know the routine by heart. Please, allow me to stop this miserable, rotten pirate myself."

Alex was about to say no, it was far too dangerous, when she noticed the faeries exchanging amused looks.

"There's no point in trying to stop him," said Carroll. "When Encore says he's going to stop an evildoer, he's made up his mind."

"Don't worry too much," said Drosselmeyer. "He's more than capable. Besides, I trained him myself. With *his* training regimen, he's nothing short of the finest fencer in the world."

In spite of their comforting words, Alex was still unsure. But there was no denying the fire in Encore's eyes, and she remembered her own actions, finding the Chronicle, building a network . . . She placed her hands on his shoulders and gave him a kiss on the forehead. "Promise me you'll be safe."

Encore nodded and gave her a smile. "Promise," he said. "I'll be back before the show starts." And with that, he was off to hunt down a pirate.

The Tempest had a spring in her step as she

made her way to the palace armory. Though she dressed the part of a dignified admiral, she was and always would be a swashbuckling pirate at heart, and just like any other buccaneer, her one true love in the world was treasure. Booty. Loot. Swag. Nothing in the world thrilled her more, and already mountains of narcisi were swirling about in her head when a voice snapped her out of her daydreams.

"Greetings, Admiral!"

The pirate turned around to find herself face to face with the Renegade Mage, hands on his hips and a smile on his face.

"You!" she hissed. "What do ye think yer doin' here in the palace? Yer not welcome here."

"Oh, on the contrary, I believe it is you who is the interloper in my palace," said the boy with a twinkle in his eye.

"What be the meaning of this nonsense?" the pirate chuckled. "You come here for death, I've got it for ya." She pulled her rapier from her belt.

"You really don't know who I am, do you?" asked the boy, unsheathing his own.

"Of course I do, yer the Renegade Mage what's been a thorn in the king's side," said the pirate.

"Aside from that," said the boy. The pirate simply tilted her head in confusion. "Well, I suppose I can't be too surprised. We hardly had a chance for proper introductions when we first met, what with you trying to kill me and all. All right, then. Allow me to take the opportunity to introduce myself. Prince Encore Corona, heir to the throne of Bellarossa."

The pirate's eyes narrowed. "So ye have been sticking those barnacles on his brain. Anyway. Can't be. I sent the whelp to the bottom o' the sea."

"Admiral Drake, he saved me." From his pocket, he flipped out a chunky chain. Unmistakably, Admiral Drake's famous chain.

The prince couldn't help but smile as he saw the pirate's eyes widen and freeze. But it was only a moment before her expression of shock was replaced with a wicked grin, and now she was raising her rapier. "Well, shiver me timbers, this ghost has blood in it yet. Don't matter, ye scurvy brat. I'm happy to kill ye again."

She stepped forward as Encore took form, and the two duelists began to close the gap between them. They advanced slowly at first, taking cautious, deliberate steps until they were within blade's reach of one another, but the duel was still yet to commence. When they finally touched blades, they did so lightly at first, with pauses in between. Then, without warning, the duel began proper, and the sound of steel clashing steel and twanging, whooshing blades filled the air.

It quickly became apparent why sailors spoke of the Tempest in the same hushed tones typically reserved for thunderstorms and hurricanes. Every thrust and lunge came with all of the devastating speed and force of a lightning bolt, and the notorious pirate was just getting started. With every passing second, she grew more and more fierce, and now she was unleashing a veritable cataclysm of steel onto the prince. Ten more thrusts, fifteen more lunges, and it was everything he could do to defend himself. But she was too swift, too strong, too ruthless. The eleventh thrust caught him off guard and pinked his shoulder. The sixteenth lunge grazed his arm and sent a few drops of crimson splattering to the ground.

"Aww ... what's the matter?" chuckled the Tempest. "Too much for a wee runt like ye to handle? Scurvy bilge rat. I'll cleave ye to the brisket! And then it's off to hunt the Faeries!"

The prince was finished now; her eyes showed she knew it. He was panting heavily, covered in sweat, and the Tempest readied her rapier for the final onslaught that would be his demise.

Or so she thought. Instead, the prince parried the attack, and leapt to his feet.

"You should have held your tongue," the prince said without a trace of his usual lightheartedness as the two duelists gauged their options. "But you just couldn't keep quiet. Well, I suppose I ought to thank you for reminding me what's at stake. All right then. Hear me now, vicious pirate. I am Encore Corona, prince of Bellarossa. And I swear on my honor to protect all of Bellarossa, Human or Faerie."

The Tempest was still reeling from the shock of the fight not being done. "Ye sure are a bold one, aren't ye, lad?" she said with a wicked smile. "Well, I suppose ye've more than earned it. I can hardly remember the last time someone gave me a proper duel. Oh, it's a shame I'll only be able to kill ye once more."

She lunged forward and the duel resumed, both combatants growing more and more determined. The prince took another thrust to the arm and retaliated with a lunge on the Tempest's shoulder. By now, the sound of steel clashing steel had swelled into a full symphony of metal, and both duelists seemed to realize that the bout was approaching its climax, one way or the other. The Tempest summoned every last drop of strength and skill she had accumulated over a lifetime of swashbuckling, but the prince executed parry after parry, thrust after thrust, lunge after lunge, and the Tempest was on the ground. With one final maneuver, he sent her blade flying and speared her magnificent, feathered tricorne, flicking it off. Now, he had his rapier at her throat, and the pirate threw up her arms in surrender.

"Not bad," she conceded with a smile. "I suppose congratulations are in order. But it's all for naught. Yer still no match for the king."

"Maybe not," said the prince, keeping his blade to her neck. "But my sister is more than capable of outwitting anyone in the world. Come along now then. We've a stop to make before the dungeon."

In the throne room, King Jean-Claude sat alone with his anxieties. Where was the smell of tarts coming from two days ago? Or the music just yesterday? King Johannes and Prince Encore were dead. Of course they were. They had to be. He knew that. And yet . . . maybe it was the Tempest's ghost stories. Maybe it was the Mage's sorcery. But everywhere he went, he felt as though he were being followed by the specter of the king. So he sat, his anxieties swirling around in his head, when he heard a most unsettling sound.

It sounded like a dog howling in the distance, and the eerie noise sent shivers down the king's spine. It only lasted for a moment before it stopped, but then it resumed, and now the music of a whole chorus of hounds was reverberating through the wide, empty walls of the throne room.

"Guards," said King Jean-Claude, barely whispering at first. "Guards!" he bellowed as he leapt to his feet and made a mad dash for the exit. He was nearly at the doors when they swung open, and in rushed a great stream of fire that engulfed the throne room in seconds, transforming it into a raging inferno.

But that wasn't even half as frightening as

what accompanied the fire. For standing amidst the flames was the sallow, lumbering figure of King Johannes.

"Jean-Claude!" King Johannes wailed as the flames swelled, and the hounds grew louder.

"Your, your Majesty!" Jean-Claude sputtered out as he stumbled to the floor, his heart nearly bursting out of his chest. "Wha—? But, but, but, how are you—?"

"Jean-Claude!" the king said again, an eerie tremor in his voice as he advanced on the former prime minister. "Who killed me? Who killed me? And who killed my son?"

At this, all the color drained from Jean-Claude's face, and he felt his blood curdle. "I-I-I, I don't know, Your Majesty! I swear!"

"Tell the truth, Jean-Claude!" King Johannes wailed as Jean-Claude tried and failed to get back on his feet. "Tell the truth!"

Jean-Claude opened his mouth, but no words escaped. All he could manage was a series of contorted gasps.

"Who killed me, Jean-Claude?" King Johannes repeated. "Tell the truth!"

"Please, Your Majesty! Please!" Jean-Claude

begged as he shuffled backwards in a desperate attempt to flee from the nightmarish vision before him. "I promise, my word; I don't know!" He glanced around the room.

King Johannes let out a frightful growl from the depths of his chest, and the flames' dance grew even more violent.

"It's just us here now, old friend. This is your last chance, Jean-Claude," he wailed. "Tell me the truth, or my spirit will never be at rest."

At this, the quivering wreck of a man gave in. "Oh, I confess, Your Majesty! It was me! I killed you! I poisoned you and had the Tempest, Admiral Allardyce, kill the prince at sea! I'm sorry, Your Majesty! Please! Have mercy on me!"

The moment he was finished, the former prime minister blacked out, and his whole body fell limp on the floor. A few moments later, the flames died down, as did the dogs' howling, and the life drained from King Johannes's body, leaving behind nothing but a carefully painted statue. The doors to the throne room swung open, and in walked quite the crowd: the princesses and the Faeries; the prince and his prisoner, now bound in steel; and several court ministers and navy officers.

"To think that Jean-Claude was the king's murderer all along," said Minister Hopkins.

"Officer," Minister Armstrong addressed a commodore. "Bring this scoundrel to the Ministry of Justice at once for detainment."

"Sir! Yes, Sir!" said the commodore. And with that, he had six soldiers handcuff the false king and lead him and the pirate away. Once they were gone, the Corona siblings and the three faeries let out a great cheer.

"Yes!" laughed Lyric. "We are the champions! Forget you, Jean-Claude!"

"Serves you right, Prime Sinister! You too, you lousy pirate!" Palette jeered.

"We did it!" Alamode gushed as she leapt for joy. "Bellarossa is free!"

"Great work painting Daddy's statue, you two," beamed Gateau. "Great work, everyone!"

"Yes, of course," said Carroll with a smile. "But let's not forget who came up with this whole plan in the first place."

"You're right!" Encore cheered. "Three cheers for Alex! The hero of Bellarossa!"

The others also cheered as they piled on Alex.

"Aww . . . thanks, everyone. You were all great,"

Alex giggled as she found herself at the center of a nine-party group hug.

And as they stood there as a family, each and every one of them felt light and free in a way that none of them had felt in a very long time. For at long last, the kingdom was free, and soon it would be restored to its true ruler.

Chapter 9:

The True Ruler
of Bellarossa

"—And with that, let the festivities commence!"

The courtyard erupted with excitement at Alex's declaration in eager anticipation of the party to come. A month had passed since the kingdom had been reclaimed, and the Corona had announced a grand celebration to commemorate the joyous occasion. Three whole days of festivities, featuring the unveiling of a new statue courtesy of Palette on the first day, followed by a showcase of Encore's theater affinity on the second, culminating on the third with Encore's coronation and his first act as king, conducting an offering ceremony at the newly refurbished Faerie Well. At first, Alex had objected to Encore being crowned at such a young age as thirteen and nominated the newly inducted Prime Minister Armstrong to act as regent in his stead until the prince turned eighteen. But the prime minister nebulously assured her that the prince had spoken with the court, and in light of the unprecedented circumstances, they had agreed that a break from tradition was well warranted. In any case, they felt that having the proper monarch of Bellarossa conduct the ceremony would send a powerful message of welcoming to the small cohort of Faeries that had come out of hiding since Jean-Claude's removal.

Yes, the Corona had made sure to make the Faeries' contributions to the kingdom's liberation well known and issued a public invitation to the Faeries to emerge from hiding and partake in the celebration, along with a commitment to further talks on how to coexist in Bellarossa. And emerge they did. At first, there were only a few of them, but one by one, more came forth, and by the time of the festival, no fewer than twenty faeries had come out of hiding and were staying in rooms at and around the palace. And just like in the days of old, they delighted in enthralling audiences with demonstrations of their wonderful powers. One of them could conjure clouds that released gentle snow showers, and another could coax plants to sprout blossoms whenever they pleased. Yet another could charm instruments to make music by themselves, and one more still could transmute water into paint. There was even a faerie who could enchant kites to make them fly without handlers and do all sorts of fantastic tricks. In addition to their eclectic acts of the arcane, these faeries were generous in doling out enchantments to the kingdom's artisans. And as they did, they seemed to help revitalize the kingdom's long-dormant creative spirit as it awoke from its nightmarish slumber.

The good people of Bellarossa, for their part, did their best to make the Faeries feel welcome, with calm but firm explanations to any who raised fear or doubt. And as Alex made her way through the crowds fraternizing in the courtyard, she felt an unmistakable sense of communion and kinship in the air. Before long, Alex arrived at her table, where her siblings and Encore's three faerie parents were eagerly awaiting her.

"Great job, Lexi!" Alamode cheered as Alex joined the group. "You were amazing up there!"

"Thanks," said Alex as everyone else offered her their praises. "And great work to you too."

The others echoed Alex's compliments. A quick glance was all one needed to see that their praise was well-deserved. Caressing each princess's figure was a dreamlike confection of linen and silk, dyed in delicate pastels. The three faeries were garbed in light tunics which seamlessly integrated their spectacular wings into the ensemble. Rounding out the party was Encore, dressed in a pristine, ivory suit and his trademark top hat. Everyone was as immaculately coiffed and made up as ever, and the talk didn't stray from clothing and makeup until the food came out.

When the banquet arrived, it took a whole parade of servers to set it up, and it was a wonder the buffet didn't collapse under the weight. In addition to the usual roasts, soups, and vegetables, the buffet also featured all manner of pastries and sweetmeats as well as a plethora of fruit dishes to cater to the Faerie palate. Enormous bowls filled with all kinds of fruit—apples and cherries and bananas and oranges and pineapples and melons and berries and grapes and peaches and pears— cut into pieces and waiting to be tossed into salads or dipped into fountains flowing with rich chocolate and caramel. Jars of thick, gooey jam and marmalade accompanying baskets brimming with brioche. Platters laden with fruit grilled by the slice or candied and arranged into colorful skewers. And for the first time in centuries, large casks of golden, bubbly faerie mead graced the banquet tables, a sheer delight to all who sampled their contents.

"So, what do you all think?" Gateau asked with a smile after everyone had sat down and had a chance to get started on the food.

"It's all wonderful, Gateau. Everything tastes amazing," Carroll said as Drosselmeyer and Tanabata nodded in agreement through mouthfuls of food.

"Really amazing," Alamode concurred. "Cory certainly seems to think so. Look at him go!"

At this, all eyes turned to the prince, whose cheeks were bulging with food. His eyes darted around, caught off guard, before he swallowed and gave everyone a sheepish grin. "Err . . . pardon my manners. I still can't believe how good everything is."

"Right," teased Palette. "As if you haven't had Gateau's cooking for a whole month now. You're in a hurry for dessert like always. Just be careful you don't choke *again*."

Everyone laughed before Lyric came to her brother's defense. "Hey, come on now. It's not his fault her desserts are the best. After all, who can mix it all with love and make the world taste good?"

Gateau felt her cheeks flush at her sister's praise but broke into a smile nonetheless. "The candy ma'am can."

Lyric flashed a smile and embraced her sister. "I'm so proud of you."

"Thanks, Lyric," said Gateau, beaming widely. "Yeah, I think it all came out really nice. Bon appétit, everyone!"

Lavish as it was, the food was but one of the festival's amenities. Decorating the courtyard were extravagant floral arrangements and opulent ice sculptures. And the transcendental stylings of the ever-diligent court orchestra accompanied the party through its every mood. Yes, the Corona had spared no effort to ensure that the party would be one befitting of such a rapturous occasion, and everyone in attendance kept the highest of spirits through it all.

Eventually, the hour arrived for the day's closing event, and Palette climbed up the stairs of the central hall terrace. At the base of the terrace rested Palette's statue, hidden from view under a massive tarp.

"Good people of Bellarossa," Palette began, "I hope you are all enjoying today's festivities."

At this point, she was interrupted by a thunderous round of cheers and applause. She waited for the crowd to settle down before continuing.

"Yes, it's been a long thirteen years, hasn't it? But at long last, the Corona have reclaimed the throne, and we can't wait to begin serving you, our people, again. But we mustn't forget who helped make this all possible. And so, without further ado, I'd like to present our new friends with a special present. Please, consider it a token of our gratitude."

With that, the tarp was lowered to reveal the likenesses of Tanabata, Drosselmeyer, and Carroll, their proudly posed figures seeming to exude an aura of raw power. At this, the applause swelled once more, and the three featured faeries fluttered upward onto the platform. For a while, they did nothing but smile and wave at the crowd before they finally spoke.

"Thank you, Your Majesty, for the lovely souvenir," said Drosselmeyer with a bright smile. "We are truly humbled to receive such a thoughtful gift."

"Yeah, and thanks for inviting us to the party!" cheered Tanabata, who couldn't help the fact that her wings were fluttering wildly with excitement.

"Indeed," said Carroll with a graceful curtsey. "May today herald the beginning of a shining new era of peace and goodwill."

Palette curtseyed in turn before rejoining the trio on center stage to share in a large hug.

After the first day of the festival had wound down to a close, and the guests had all left to get a good night's rest, the Corona siblings and the faeries were all sitting at the base of the terrace steps admiring Palette's sculpture.

"Sweet statue," Lyric offered as she admired the faeries' sculpted features.

"Definitely," nodded Alex. "It gives you a sense

of optimism for a future where Humans and Faeries can coexist in harmony."

No sooner had she finished her sentence than a great ball of brilliant, white light materialized in the air and slowly descended. When it reached the ground, the light dissipated to reveal a most incredible sight. Floating before everyone was a faerie maiden of ethereal beauty sporting a crown of blossoms and a magnificent pair of prismatic wings. Accompanying her were four more faeries who carried themselves with an air of dignity befitting a royal court.

"Good royals of Bellarossa," she began, an unmistakable cadence of nobility to her voice. "And good Fae too. Please, pardon me for arriving unannounced. I've heard so much about your efforts to protect my subjects, I simply had to pay a visit to express my gratitude. Oh, but first, allow me to introduce myself. My name is Titania. Titania Odette. My great grandmother Titania Rampion appeared before your king groom and his faerie bride centuries ago to offer them a wedding present in thanks for their hospitality to our own. Exceptional powers of artistry for all children of the land who wish it, and seek to find their affinity. I am Queen of the Faeries."

"Well met, Your Majesty," said Alex as she dropped into a deep curtsey, the others following her lead. "We humbly accept your words of gratitude. It is our great honor and privilege to carry out this mission of goodwill."

"Yes, quite," said the Faerie Queen with a faint smile. But from the look in her eyes, Alex could tell something was amiss.

"Your Majesty," Alex began cautiously. "Is something the matter?"

"It is," began the Faerie Queen. "Faeries have been told before of plans to coexist, but always under the benevolence of a human king, always sealed on cold symbolic structures, always within the narrow paths of lineage. As you have seen, these human traditions have bound the multitudes to the greed of the few. For the Fae, we have Kings and Queens and Kwins and it is the spirit of their affinity which finds them in leadership, not the line of their blood. We have a saying."

"Family is heart, not blood," Encore was heard to say. "I'm sorry to interrupt. My parents taught me."

The Queen smiled so warmly. "Yes, child, that is it. We do not seek to dictate your ways, but it is a difficult celebration for us, wishing to gain your view and trust, yet knowing we must live in these new, unfamiliar settings, rather than in the forests of old. Knowing we are freer, but not free. Yes, some may choose to live here, but if there were a patch of forest for our own, where we could rebuild our own ways, it would ease our strain. A haven also for unsettled Fae seeking respite from or not ready for the shared areas."

"Hmm," Alex mused as she nodded in understanding. But what could she offer? Encore as king could order a patch of forest, but she remembered being confined to her tower. There was no amount of finery or gifts that had made up for not being able to travel the land. And she, too, had held her tongue against the source holding power. She gazed at her brother, seeing the worry in his eyes. Perhaps, they were thinking much of the same things.

"I have ideas, if you will offer me the grace of time to consider them."

"Of course." The Queen and her entourage gave

a kindly yet curt nod, and floated back away into the night sky.

The following morning, Alex and Encore got up early to head to the courtyard before the day's festivities got started. They had important business to tend to, but given how small and familiar of an assembly they had called, they felt they could stand to hold the meeting in a more casual setting than within the gilded walls of the assembly chamber.

It wasn't long before Nonno Pumpkinseed—one of the two individuals Alex had specifically invited—arrived, with Harvest tagging along.

"Princess Alexandria," greeted Nonno Pumpkinseed. "My, how you've grown. I don't believe I've seen you since you came to Corno Verde for the opening of that library thirteen years ago."

Alex smiled. Nonno Pumpkinseed was right. Though she had caught a glimpse of him amidst the crowds the day prior, she was too busy overseeing the party to have a chance to sit down with him and have a proper conversation. And setting that aside, they hadn't seen each other since his days as governor. Back then, he used to be a regular visitor at the palace, whether on business or simply to see his good friend, King Johannes. And now, seeing him properly for the first time in thirteen years, Alex felt a wave of nostalgia come over her, and she giggled a delirious little giggle.

"Good to see you too," said Alex, not even bothered by his addressing her by her formal name. "How have you been?"

"I've been well," said Nonno Pumpkinseed. "Glad to be in the final group to see the walls of those dreary dungeons, even if Jean-Claude and Allardyce don't really deserve their own private island, speck or not. But enough of them. I've been spending my time tending the farm when I'm not busy with my duties as governor. Speaking of which, I just realized I haven't had the chance to thank you for that yet."

"Of course," said Alex. "We weren't about to let Governor Scallion stay in office. After his dismissal, the court knew exactly who to appoint to the vacant position. And it didn't hurt that a certain *someone* gave you a glowing recommendation."

Encore chuckled before quipping, "Guilty as charged."

"I still can't believe you were the Renegade Mage all along," said Harvest. "*And* the lost prince on top of that. And you still came by to see me after learning the truth."

"Of course I did," said Encore with a bright smile. "I wasn't just going to leave you, especially not after they took Nonno away."

"I'm just glad he made it out all right," said Alex with a grin. "Not that I'm at all surprised. It's like Lyric was saying just yesterday. There's no smashing this pumpkin."

That got a chuckle out of everyone. Not quite a hearty, boisterous laugh, but rather the cathartic, comfortable sort of mirth of someone having just come out of a great ordeal. They calmed down when another figure came to join them, escorted by the palace guards.

"Hello, Alex," greeted Maple with a smile. "Good to see you."

"Hello, Maple," said Alex. "Good to see you too. I hope the tree farm has been doing well."

"It's been marvelous," sighed Maple. "It's so nice to walk through the trees again and breathe in that familiar, woody air. Thank you so much for returning my family's farm to me."

"Of course," said Alex. "We certainly weren't going to keep it. Yet, the royal arborists are yours for as long as you need them. Which brings me to the reason I summoned you here today."

"Pardon me, Your Majesty," said the captain of the guards. "Before you begin, Prime Minister Armstrong has been looking for the prince all morning. He said they had one more rehearsal scheduled before the day's festivities got started."

"Whoops, I forgot all about that," said Encore. "I should probably head on over. Wouldn't want to mess up my first formal performance. Don't worry, Sis. I trust you to preside over today's meeting yourself."

"Are you sure?" asked Alex as Encore started for the guards.

"Absolutely," said Encore with a smile and a wave. "Come on, Harvest. Want an early, private viewing of the show?"

With that, the two boys followed the guards away, leaving Alex with Nonno Pumpkinseed and Maple.

"All right then," said Alex. "I suppose now's as good a time as any to begin."

She took a moment to collect her thoughts before starting. "As you are no doubt aware, for the past month, the Corona have been campaigning for amicable relations with the Fae and offering asylum to its refugees. Well, just yesterday, the Palace of Bellarossa was visited by the Faerie Queen herself. And during her visit, it became clear to me that concepts of benevolence and asylum presume these lands are ours to lord over in the first place, not ours to share. Faeries deserve a home. They, as you know, have traditionally lived in the woods. I wished we could offer something returned. Somewhere with lots of trees as well as a healthy crop of fruit and sugarcane. Unfortunately, there's no place in the kingdom like that that isn't already largely settled by people, and our efforts to move people will take time."

Now, Alex could see a spark of realization begin to glimmer in Nonno Pumpkinseed's and Maple's eyes.

"And so, the court of Bellarossa has set aside a land grant on the border of Corno Verde and

Passo Legna for something I like to call the Faerie Habitat Restoration Project. It is the court's goal to transform this land into a safe haven for the preservation and reparation of the Fae civilization. The project will be a lot of work, no doubt, but richly rewarding for its undertakers. Of course, we'll need an experienced farmer and an experienced arborist to help oversee the project, not under leadership of the Human crown, but under the Faerie Queen. I thought to myself that there could be no one better suited to the task in all the kingdom than the steadfast governor of Corno Verde and the valiant proprietor of the Maple Family Tree Farm. That is, if they're willing."

For a moment, no one said a word, then Nonno Pumpkinseed broke the silence.

"It won't be easy," he chuckled. "But I suppose nothing worth doing ever is. I'd be honored to help however I can, as long as the Queen will have me."

"As would I," said Maple with a smile. "Rest assured, Princess. We'll see this through no matter what. You can count on it."

Alex smiled. "I know I can." And with that, she entered day two of the festival in the highest of spirits.

The second afternoon was filled with every bit as much fun and excitement as the first, even more when the procession carrying Queen Cinnamon, the siblings' aunt, arrived, beaming with tears and hugs, having had a message carried to her royal docks, delivered by a chirping dolphin. The note had explained that a false king had prevented messages from reaching her, and let her know that her nephew was not only alive, but set for a coronation. The plump, regal woman was quickly surrounded by elder palace staff and ministers who were thrilled to see her here and in good health after so many years, and, almost before anyone realized it, the hour had arrived for the day's closing event.

Everyone was happy to interrupt any catching up for this, as everyone had been looking forward to Encore's premier performance as the prince proper. Presently, Lyric was perched on the central hall terrace as her brother's opening act, while Encore and his parents waited in the central hall.

"Encore," Drosselmeyer's voice called out.

Hearing his name, the boy turned his attention away from his extravagantly colorful outfit and towards the sapphire-winged faerie.

"What's the matter? You've been acting restless ever since Lyric got on stage. Are you okay?"

"He's nervous about performing," said Tanabata before turning to the boy. "Aren't you?"

Encore exhaled and let out a nervous chuckle. "A little bit," he confessed. "It's my first real show. There's a lot at stake here."

"Encore," said Carroll. "Surely you're not *too* scared. You who have risked your life time and time again to save lives and help liberate the kingdom. There is no grade for this, no competition, no victory, but for the bringing of joy."

"Yeah," chuckled Drosselmeyer. "Come on, Encore. This is nothing compared to some of your previous stunts."

"You're going to do great," promised Tanabata. "We *know* you will."

"And no matter what happens," said Carroll as she placed a hand on Encore's shoulder. "You'll always be our little circus performer."

For a moment, Encore continued to mull

over his worries, but then he exhaled again and smiled as he adjusted his ivory top hat. "Thanks, everyone."

At this point, the four of them could hear the crowds applauding outside, and now Lyric was ambling up to them, guitar in hand.

"You're up, Bro," she said with a smile. "Get out there, and show them what you can do."

The crowds were already going wild when Encore emerged onto the terrace.

"Good afternoon, everyone!" he bellowed, stoking the crowd's already hot passions. "How are you all doing today? I'd like to thank each and every one of you for being a part of today's festival. And now, without further ado, prepare yourselves for the greatest circus the world has ever seen!"

The prince never took his promises lightly, and the show that followed did not disappoint. From the dancing lights that sparkled like fireworks to the vivid choreography of the marionettes to the whimsical tricks of the volunteering animals. The audience *oohed* and *aahed* at it all, and Alex had the biggest smile on her face as her sisters laughed and cheered with delight. And when a final spectacle of colored lights marked the end of the show,

Alex stood up and cheered along with the rest of the courtyard. And as she brought her hands together in applause, she found herself thinking, *tomorrow's the big day.*

The following afternoon, the Corona siblings stepped out of the coach that had brought them to the Faerie Well, where the coronation was to be conducted. With its refurbished roof, polished walls, and thriving garden, the Faerie Well really was a very handsome monument, and Alex couldn't help but take a moment to admire it while people were setting everything up. But it wasn't long before her thoughts were interrupted.

"Lexi?"

The princess turned to see Alamode motioning towards some nearby bushes.

"Come on over? Cory wanted to talk with all of us about something."

"You think he's nervous about his coronation?" Alex asked as Alamode led the way.

"Mm . . . not quite," said Alamode.

A short walk later, the two of them found themselves in a clearing where their brother and sisters were waiting. Encore smiled and saluted to acknowledge their arrival.

"Hey," said Alex. "What's the matter? Alamode says there's something on your mind."

"Yes, well," Encore began, pausing for a moment before continuing. "You see . . . I've been thinking. About ascending the throne. And the thing is, I grew up in a forest without much to ever take care of. And I just don't think I'm ready for all of the formality and responsibility that comes with being king."

"Fair enough," said Alex. "If you're getting cold feet, we can ask Prime Minister Armstrong to act as regent until you come of age."

"That's an option," said Encore. "But I think we already have someone who would make a very capable ruler. Someone wise and brave with a heart full of love."

"Who?" asked Alex. For a moment, she could only give Encore an uncomprehending stare until she realized what he meant.

"You . . . You don't mean . . . ?"

Encore nodded, his smile never leaving his

face. Around them, their sisters were all smiling as well.

"No, I couldn't," she managed to say. "Bellarossa has only ever had kings."

"So?" said Encore. "Why should that matter? People here love and respect you. If I didn't know better, I'd think that was more important than who you were born from."

"Well, I . . ." Alex fumbled for words as she turned from one face to another.

"The court has signed the order: a monarch does not need to be a king. I took the crown in a private ceremony, signed it, and then stepped down. Now the prime minister will look to you first, to see if you'll accept."

"Encore," Alex breathed out, surprised by how bold her brother really could be.

"Just make sure you have an heir," Lyric said in a hesitantly joking tone. "Or if something happens to you, that crown will pass to me, and I just want to play music. I'd pass it to Alamode."

"I *would* be a beautiful queen," Alamode mused.

Alex paused. Her sister was kind and talented, but had never struck her as the type to lead.

"Alex will be fine," Gateau reassured them all. "I think you would make an excellent ruler. You just have to believe in yourself."

"Yeah," said Lyric. "Why should what you were born as matter to who you are?"

"You better not let us down, Sis," said Palette, with a playful grin.

"See?" said Encore. "Everyone's okay with it. The court has given its approval as well. But we won't force you. It's only if you accept."

But Alex was still staring at Lyric, barely hearing a voice from behind her.

"Um, Lexi?" said Alamode. Alex turned to see her sister holding a pillow upon which rested a golden tiara.

"Cory told me what he was planning a few weeks ago and asked me to make this for you. You could use it as your tiara, if you like it. If you do accept his offer."

Alex examined the beautiful headpiece for a good minute or two, neither laying a finger on it nor saying a word, before she looked around at everyone's faces one more time and nodded.

"Okay. I'll do it."

"What was that?" asked Encore with a smile.

"I said I'll do it!" Alex proclaimed. Her siblings all cheered for her, and they made their way back to the Faerie Well where a large, wooden staircase and pulley system had been set up in front of the monument.

"Well?" asked a smiling Minister Hopkins. "What did she say?"

"I said I'll ascend the throne," said Alex with a confident smile.

"Wonderful," said Minister Hopkins. "I'm sure you'll make your father proud. Come on then, the prime minister is waiting for you."

With that, Alex was led to the base of the stairs before an audience composed of Nonno Pumpkinseed, Harvest and his friends, Maple, and the Faerie Queen, as well as hundreds of humans and faeries, her brother and sisters standing off to the side along with Cory's parents and Queen Cinnamon. The crowd seemed somewhat confused to see Alex and not Encore, but no one raised any objections. After a lot of pomp and circumstance, the crowning moment finally arrived, and Prime Minister Armstrong proclaimed for all to hear, "I present to you your new ruler, Queen Alexandria Corona!"

For a moment, the crowd was silent. But then, slowly, they began to applaud. And as they did, their applause grew louder and louder until it surpassed any ovation Alex had ever heard.

"Hail to the queen!" someone proclaimed. "Long may she reign!"

"The people of Bellarossa are behind you!" cried another voice.

"May you bring prosperity to us all!" cheered someone else.

As the people's overwhelming words of faith resounded in Alex's ears, she couldn't help but fill with delight.

"Thank you for your support, everyone," she said, once the crowds had finally settled down. "It warms my heart to know that you all have such confidence in me. There will be many changes to come, that will center wellbeing for all, safety for all, and . . . choice." She had new, sprouting ideas. Bold ideas. But she would first talk to her court. Talk to the governors. Talk to her siblings. Ask the Faerie Queen for her counsel. Speaking of which. "And now, for my first act as queen, let us conduct a final offering ceremony at the Faerie Well, after which it will be maintained as a memorial."

With that, a team of four carried an enormous bowl of fruit and sugarcane up to the well and placed it on the pedestal. Alex was about to place her hands on the pedestal when she had an idea. "Hey!" she called to her siblings. "Come on over here!"

For a moment, her siblings just exchanged looks of surprise—as did the rest of her audience—before they got up and joined Alex.

"Come on then," she said. "Everyone put your hands on the offering stone with me."

Her siblings' eyes went wide.

"But this is *your* ceremony," Palette began. "We're not supposed to—"

"Oh, who cares about that silly old tradition?" said Alex. "We'll make new and better ones. You're my family. I couldn't have saved the kingdom without you. And I want you all here beside me now."

For a moment, no one moved a muscle or said a word. But then, one by one, each of the Corona siblings placed their hands on the offering pedestal and followed Alex's lead as she began to chant:

Tired, poor, hungry faeries, rest your weary souls

Come and stay; rest and repose; so that you may feel whole

And as Alex looked around to see her siblings' glowing faces, she could feel herself welling up with optimism from the bottom of her heart. For in that moment, the future seemed full of promise, and Alex couldn't wait to write a new shining chapter in the story of Bellarossa.

About the Author
Jubilee Cho

Jubilee Cho (she/her) [1998-2024] is a fairy tale writer from Anaheim, California, who will always be a princess at heart, and offers you this book as a gift, in joy, solidarity, and hope. May you find a world full of magic.

www.ingramcontent.com/pod-product-compliance
Lightning Source LLC
Chambersburg PA
CBHW020751310726

48969CB00002B/494